# WITH A BARE BODKIN
### by CYRIL HARE

"The naturalness of the story is emphasized by the abandonment of that moth-eaten convention of the amateur investigator. Mr. Hare's detectives are ordinary policemen, neither over-wise nor cocksure, and in Mr. Pettigrew he has an extra observer, a man of charm and understanding who is a genuine character creation...."

—*The Spectator*

CYRIL HARE

# *With a Bare Bodkin*

PERENNIAL LIBRARY
Harper & Row, Publishers
New York, Cambridge, Hagerstown, Philadelphia, San Francisco
London, Mexico City, São Paulo, Sydney

*To*

F.F.G.C.

*'the onlie begetter . . .'*

A hardcover edition of this book was originally published by Faber & Faber Ltd. It is here reprinted by arrangement.

First PERENNIAL LIBRARY edition published 1980.

ISBN: 0-06-080523-4

    81 82 83 84 10 9 8 7 6 5 4 3 2

# CONTENTS

# CHAPTER ONE

## *Pettigrew Goes North*

FRANCIS PETTIGREW was staring gloomily out of the window of his chambers in the Temple at the trees on the Embankment and the grey glimmer of the river beyond them. It was by no means an unattractive view, but it displeased him. He was a man of conservative temperament and for twenty years he had been accustomed to having his vision bounded by a sober red brick wall twenty paces distant. Two months previously one high explosive bomb and a handful of incendiaries had opened up the vista by removing the red brick wall and the two blocks of buildings beyond it. For the first time since they were built, the chambers were now exposed to the full light of day. There was, Pettigrew felt, something rather indecent about it.

He sighed and turned from the window to the man standing in the room behind him.

'Well, there you are,' he said. 'It's yours, for the duration. Apart from the gap in the ceiling, the place isn't in bad order. I should be careful how you handle the books, though. Some of them are pretty filthy. The Meeson and Welsbys in the corner, especially, had most of the soot from the chimney next door driven into them. And of course there's always the chance of a glass splinter here and there. You're not bringing many books of your own, I suppose?'

The other man grinned.

'Not very many,' he said. 'One odd volume of Halsbury, to be precise. I happened to have taken it home with me the night of the blitz. It's almost the only existing relic of Mulberry Court of blessed memory. Really it's very good of you to let me take this place over. I can't imagine what I should have done if——'

'Say no more about it, old boy. It's a kindness on your part to keep the chambers warm while I'm away.'

'When do you go?'

'Tonight as ever is. I feel a bit of a fool launching out on a new job at my time of life, but they really seemed to want me to do it and I felt I oughtn't to turn it down.'

'What is the job, exactly? One of these Ministries, I suppose?'

Pettigrew assumed an expression of deep solemnity.

'The Pin Control,' he said portentously. Then, 'Ever heard of it?'

'Er — yes, I think so. It looks after the pin trade, I suppose?'

'So far as I have been able to find out, that is a very inadequate description of its activities. The gentleman whom I saw about the job — he was no less a person than the Controller's own deputy assistant director, mark you — he gave me to understand in no uncertain terms that on the proper administration of the Pin Control hinged the entire — I forget how he put it, but I assure you it made a deep impression on me, more than pin-deep I was going to say, but perhaps that would be an exaggeration. And as Legal Adviser to the Control, I am going to be a person of some consequence. Just how consequential you may discover if you care to glance at that masterpiece of light literature, the Pin Restrictions (No. 3) Order, 1940 — but I don't advise you to, unless you have to.'

'I don't see why you shouldn't do your advising from the Temple.'

'Neither, to be perfectly frank, do I. But the Pin

Control is established at Marsett Bay, and so to Marsett Bay I go.'

'Marsett Bay. Let me see, where exactly is that?'

'You may well ask. It's somewhere on the Polar Circuit, I'm given to understand. In the very depths – no, even worse than that, on the very fringes of what Shakespeare so justly described as our nook-shotten island. Anyhow, there's a ticket to the place in my pocket, and, by the same token, if I don't get a move on now, I shall miss my train. So long, old boy. Take care of the chambers. If the chimney smokes, which it always does in an east wind, you will find the best plan is to open the further window six inches at the bottom and leave the door slightly ajar. The smoke will then be diverted into the clerk's room next door, which is a great improvement, unless you have a particularly important client waiting outside. I'll write and let you know how I get on. I might even send you a card of black-market pins.'

Unlike most people who promise to write and say how they get on, Pettigrew was as good as his word. His tenant received his first letter within a fortnight of his departure to Marsett Bay.

'Dear Bill,' he wrote, 'did you ever dream that you dwelt in marble halls? If so, you will not need any description of this place. It was, I gather, decreed as a stately pleasure dome by the first and – luckily – last Lord Eglwyswrw, who made his pile (appropriately enough, in pin tables) just before the war. He chose this really lovely, but confoundedly breezy, site overlooking the sea, to plant this monstrous structure. How anybody can have seriously proposed to live in such bloated magnificence, I can't imagine. Perhaps nobody really could – at least, his lordship died within a couple of months of making the attempt, since when it stood empty until some genius realized that the marble halls were simply ideal for accommodating platoons of typists and that the endless marble corridors were just made for female messengers to run clattering down with files, or more often teapots, in their hands.

'I am fairly fortunate in having a reasonably quiet and small room to myself, intended, I should imagine, as an abode for one of the upper servants. In an even smaller cubby-hole next door is my young lady secretary. She seems to be perfectly efficient, has no conversation, thank heaven! – dumb, or merely shy? I haven't discovered yet – with the kind of face that once seen, is never remembered. Anyhow, in view of some of the women about the place – and I never imagined how positively cumbered with women the place would be – I have reason to be thankful for my Miss Brown.

'As to the other people in this shop, I haven't had the time to sort them out yet. There is the Controller, of course. He dwells in Olympian seclusion in Lord Eglwyswrw's library. I think that he would be quite a reasonable human being, if it weren't for the fact that he is a Senior Civil Servant, lent for the duration by the Treasury to run this racket. But as it is, I find him rather heavy going. In a show like this, full of amateurs and temporaries like myself, he finds few to praise and very few to speak to. Poor devil! I suppose he'll get a C.B. or something out of it at the end of the war, but he'll have earned it hardly.

'The only people I have got to know at all well are the ones who live at the residential club, alias boarding-house, which is sheltering me. They are all brother or sister pin controllers, and I think I shall get some fun out of watching their antics. Besides Miss Brown – no fun to be expected there, though – there is an odd creature named Honoria Danville, whose principal function in office hours appears to be the brewing of tea – easily the most important event of the day, I need not say. She is rather deaf, elderly, amiable and, I should say, distinctly batty. Also one Miss Clarke, a female gorgon, who rules a department with appalling efficiency and scares the life out of me.

'As for the men of the party, there is a positively poisonous young gentleman named Rickaby; a decent middle-aged ex-solicitor's-clerk, whom I suspect of having designs on Miss B. (you may remember him, by the way – weren't Mayhew and Tillotsons clients of yours? Name of Phillips); and a horn-rimmed creature called Edelman, whom I can't make head or tail of, except that he's extremely clever and a first-rate bridge player.

'I won't bore you with any further descriptions, but I have made one rather amusing discovery. An unassuming little man by the name of Wood turns out to be no other than the detective story writer Amyas Leigh. I'm sure you've come across some of his stuff – some of it quite entertaining, though his ideas of criminal procedure are pretty wild. Apparently he has been here some time quite incognito, and he was positively pink with embarrassment when I unmasked him. He ought to get some good local colour here, anyhow. The place would make quite a good setting for a homicide.

'By the way, is it really true that they are proposing to put Burroughs J. up to the Court of Appeal? I should have thought – –'

The rest of the letter was of purely forensic interest.

# CHAPTER TWO

## *A Plot is Propounded*

THE discovery that Mr Wood 'wrote' had, in fact, caused the liveliest interest among the inhabitants of the Fernlea Residential Club. It was, it must be admitted, an interest for the most part untempered by any knowledge of the works of Amyas Leigh. Each member of the little society, however, felt it necessary at least to give some explanation for not having hitherto read them. Miss Clarke 'had very little time for reading', which in view of the concentrated effort that she put into the work of harrying her subordinates was scarcely surprising. Outside office hours her sole interest was in the cinema, and she keenly resented the fact that Marsett Bay's one picture-house could only manage a change of programme once a week. Miss Danville, on the other hand, had plenty of time for reading. She was seldom seen without a book in her hand, but it was nearly always the same one – a small leather-covered tome, the title of which could not be discovered. But it was easy enough to tell from her expression as she read that it was devotional. In the circumstances it was natural that she too was ignorant of 'Death on the Bakerloo', 'The Clue of the Twisted Cravat' and the other Amyas Leigh titles. But rather unexpectedly she seemed genuinely distressed at the fact. 'I used to be very fond of thrillers,' she explained, 'but nowadays I've got out of the way of *that* kind of reading' – and she cast her eyes down again on the leather-covered book. Miss Brown, when appealed to, merely shook her head, and nobody, least of all the modest Wood, could have had the heart to expect an explanation from one so young, so shy and so obviously overcome by meeting an author in the flesh.

The men, too, made no admission of having contributed anything to Mr Wood's royalties. Mr Edelman, at the mention of the *nom de plume*, looked fixedly at its owner for a moment, murmured "Fraid not', and cut for deal. Mild, bald Mr Phillips, anxious to be polite, assured him that he must have read them all – he got all the detective stories from the library. Unfortunately, he could never remember their titles or the names of their authors, or, as it appeared, their plots. Rickaby's views on the subject were not heard. He was out that evening, a fact for which his fellow lodgers were grateful. This left Pettigrew as the sole acknowledged representative of the Amyas Leigh public. He had, in fact, qualified for this position by having reviewed his last two productions for a legal journal, and remembering the pains that he had taken to demonstrate the many technical errors into which the author had fallen, he felt thankful that the reviews had been unsigned.

But it was insisted by all, and with particular emphasis by the ladies, that no time should be lost in acquiring and reading all Mr Wood's works. Even Miss Danville, prepared to be mundane for once, was quite firm on the point. It would make it so much more interesting, she observed, to read a book when you knew the author – a sentiment to which Miss Brown murmured her incoherent agreement. Here, however, a difficulty arose. Amyas Leigh was not exactly a best-seller. Modestly, Mr Wood pointed out that at the moment his books were not readily obtainable. The shortage of paper had, in fact, constrained his publishers to take them off the market altogether. The war made it very difficult for authors. One might, of course, always pick up a copy by chance. No, the bookshop in Marsett Bay had not got any. As a matter of fact, he had glanced at their shelves only the other day. No – this was in answer to Miss Clarke – he had not had anything filmed yet. Hollywood hadn't shown any interest in him so far. Of course, one never knew, but they had so many books to choose from – –

His audience sighed in disappointment. To have an author in their midst was something, but an author whose authorship one had to take on trust was hardly the real thing.

It was the Merry Widow who provided the obvious solution.

The Merry Widow was Mrs Hopkinson. She had been at school with Miss Clarke, a fact which emboldened her to treat that formidable woman with a lack of respect, a positive flippancy, that nobody else in the entire Control would have dared to emulate. Astonishingly, Miss Clarke not only tolerated her, but enjoyed her society. They lunched together almost every day, visited the cinema together regularly each week and, out of office hours, called each other by their Christian names. 'Breezy' was the adjective that best described Mrs Hopkinson. She was, to use her own phrase, 'always on the go'. To her natural good looks, which she had done her best to spoil by tinting her hair to an alarming shade of bronze, she added an inexhaustible fund of vitality and a vulgar good humour that was hard to resist. Her age, as she was wont to announce with peals of laughter, was exactly thirty-nine.

On the particular evening when Mr Wood's double personality was disclosed, she had 'dropped in', as she often did, for a chat with Miss Clarke and had stayed for a rubber of bridge. Her interest in the subject was, of course, intense. While the game was in progress, she said little, but it was obvious from her play, which was even more slapdash than usual, that her mind was not on the cards. The moment that the rubber was over, she rose from the table with hardly a word of apology to the hapless Edelman who had partnered her. She had the air of someone who had come to a great decision.

'I've got it!' she announced. 'Listen, everybody! Mr Wood is going to write another book.'

'Well, I hope to, of course,' said Mr Wood mildly. 'But I really haven't the time for writing nowadays. The work here is – –'

'Now, now, Mr Wood!' said the Merry Widow archly. 'Hear me out. You're going to write another book – and it will be all about us!'

'But Mrs Hopkinson, *please*!' Mr Wood was writhing with embarrassment. 'I couldn't! I've never put living people into my books. One doesn't write that way. At least, I don't. It's impossible to explain, but – well, it's – –'

'Oh, I don't mean about poor little us as we really are, of course! That would be too dreadful, I'm sure. We should all be disguised, naturally – with perhaps a teeny bit of our worst selves peeping out to make it more interesting. And then we should all have the fun of reading it afterwards and guessing who was who. You'd have lots of readers, you can be sure.'

'Lots of libel actions too, I dare say,' Pettigrew murmured. Mr Wood groaned.

'But seriously,' Miss Clarke's deep voice put in, 'would not the Control make a very suitable setting for one of your stories, Mr Wood? I've always understood that these murder mysteries usually took place in a large house with a lot of people in it, so as to make the solution as difficult as possible. Here you have a very large house with a great number of people in it. I should have thought it was exactly what you wanted.'

'Well, yes,' Mr Wood admitted. 'I don't mind saying that that point had occurred to me. Of course, when you are in the way of writing you can't help looking out for backgrounds that would come in handy.'

'Then you *are* writing a book about us!' Mrs Hopkinson exclaimed in triumph. 'You see, I knew you wouldn't be able to help it!'

'No, no! I never said anything of the sort. I have no idea of writing at the moment. I only said that I agreed with Miss Clarke in thinking that the Control would make quite a good background for a book. Given the time to write it – and the plot of course,' he added.

'I'm sure plots come easy to *you*,' said Mrs Hopkinson with a dazzling smile.

'I assure you they don't always.'

'But we'd help you with that, wouldn't we?' She appealed to the room. 'Let's make a start now. Who should we have for the murderer?'

'You want to settle who's going to be murdered first, don't you?' said Mr Edelman, looking up for the first time from the newspaper to which he had retreated as soon as the rubber was over.

'Which do you think of first, Mr Wood,' the Merry Widow asked, 'the murderer or the poor slaughtered victim?'

'Oh really, I couldn't tell you,' said the harassed author. 'I've never asked myself. You can't have a murderer without someone to murder, after all. It's like the hen and the egg.'

'Is it true you always write the last chapter first?' Miss Danville asked.

'Certainly not. How can you tell what the end of a book is going to be before you've begun it?'

'Do you mean to tell me,' said Miss Clarke in a severely disapproving tone, 'that you will start a book of this kind without knowing what the solution is going to be?'

'That's not what I said at all. I only meant – –'

'Order, order!' Mrs Hopkinson clapped her hands. 'We're wandering from the giddy point. The question is, who do we want to have murdered?'

It was Mr Phillips who was actually the first person to say, 'Rickaby', but Mr Edelman, Miss Clarke, and Miss Brown were so close behind him that the name came out almost in chorus.

'Splendid! That's one thing settled right away. Now who – –'

'Wait a minute.' In spite of himself, it was obvious that Mr Wood was becoming interested. It was as though Amyas Leigh was beginning to stir beneath the disguise of the self-effacing temporary civil servant. 'Wait a minute. I'm not sure that I want to murder Rickaby.'

'Not want to murder – ? But Mr Wood, dear, why not? We all want to. He's such a ghastly person.'

'No, no. I'm not talking about my personal feelings. I'm speaking as a novelist. I just don't see Rickaby as a murderee, that's all. He's not – how shall I put it? – not *important* enough. I always like to have some central figure, on whom you can focus a mass of different motives – jealousies, hates and fears and so on. Then you have something to work on. A little wretch whom everybody dislikes isn't good enough.'

'I'm old-fashioned,' Pettigrew observed. 'Give me the millionaire's body in the library, and I'm quite content.'

Wood gave him an understanding look.

'Exactly,' he said slowly. 'Now we are getting somewhere. Do you see what I see?'

Pettigrew smiled and nodded.

'What are you two talking about?' the Merry Widow asked in exasperation. 'We haven't got a millionaire in this outfit!'

'But we have a very beautiful library,' said Pettigrew.

Wood was filling his pipe with an air of immense concentration.

'Two entrances and french windows opening on to the terrace,' he murmured. 'I noticed it the first time I went in there. It's ideal.'

Mrs Hopkinson looked from one to the other in bewilderment, and then light suddenly came to her and she clapped her hands.

'The Controller!' she exclaimed. 'Why didn't we think of it sooner? Of course! We'll blooming well massacre the Controller!'

'Really!' said Miss Clarke in her office voice, the voice that was wont to spread alarm and despondency through her entire department. 'A joke's a joke, I know, Alice, but I have to consider office discipline, and this is – –'

'Now Judith, if you are going to wet-blanket our fun and games, I'll never speak to you again! This is out of office hours and we can say what we like. Besides, Mr Wood is a real author, and if he says the Controller's to be murdered then murdered he will be. Now, who shall we have for murderer?'

'This is rather like Nuts in May, isn't it?' said Phillips.

'Rather!' Mrs Hopkinson giggled. 'Who shall we have to fetch him away, fetch him away, fetch – –'

But Miss Danville had risen to her feet.

'If you'll excuse me, I think I shall go to bed,' she said, breathlessly but determinedly. 'I don't like this – this discussion of taking the life of a fellow human being. Even in fun. It's – it's not seemly. Especially just now. When so many men and women are being sacrificed all over the world. I know I was to blame, too – I joined in this game, thoughtlessly. But when it comes to selecting one of us to play the part of Cain – – You must excuse me.'

She walked out of the room with dignity, clutching her little leather-covered book in her hand.

There was a moment's silence following her departure, and then Miss Brown's soft voice was heard.

'Oh, *poor* Miss Danville!' she murmured in a tone of genuine pity.

Pettigrew could not but notice the look of sympathy and admiration that Phillips gave her at that moment. It was obvious that, whether he shared her feelings or not, the little secretary's kindheartedness had moved him.

'Damn it! I believe he really cares for her!' thought Pettigrew. The reflection disturbed him. Miss Brown, he felt, was not the type to take a love affair lightly. It would ruin her efficiency as a secretary, and he was fully aware of her value to him.

Miss Danville had no other sympathizers.

'I expect we shall all be well and truly prayed for to-night,' said Miss Clarke contemptuously. She seemed to have conquered any distaste which she might have originally felt for the proposal, for she added, 'Go on, Alice.'

'Where was I? Oh, yes, of course, looking for a murderer. Who can we find who's a really villainous, bloodthirsty piece of work? I don't mind saying I have a certain person in my mind's eye – –'

'If you mean Rickaby,' said Mr Wood authoritatively, watching his pipe smoke curl upwards to the ceiling, 'he's no good at all.'

'Oh, Mr Wood, have a heart!' the Merry Widow groaned.

'But he isn't,' the novelist persisted. 'You've just given the reason yourself. If a man is obviously the sort you'd expect at sight to commit a crime, you can't have him for the villain of a detective story. If you do, where's

your puzzle? What you want, of course, is the most unlikely person you can find.'

'I have some little experience of this sort of thing in
real life,' Pettigrew remarked. 'And there, I find, the
police nearly always pick on the obvious person. And it
is distressing to observe that they are nearly always
right.'

'We're not getting anywhere,' complained Mrs Hopkinson. 'Look how late it is! I'll have to be toddling in
five minutes and I know I shan't sleep if we haven't
settled this. Mr Wood, who is it to be?'

'That's exactly what I've been trying to make up my
mind about. You want somebody unexpected. Well,
that, I think, would apply to any of us here. The difficulty is to find a plausible motive for murdering the
Controller, and motive is half the battle in these things.'

'We'd all like to murder him sometimes,' said Edelman.

'Of course, but that isn't quite what I meant. We'd all
be suspects, naturally. Anyone in the Control could be.
There's no reason why one should confine oneself to
the people in this room.' He paused, and then added,
'No, if I had to choose a villain, I should be rather inclined to select Miss Danville.'

'Oh, but that's unkind!' exclaimed Miss Brown im-
pulsively.

'My dear child, this is only a game,' said Miss Clarke
reprovingly.

'Miss Danville,' Mr Wood repeated. 'I don't know
whether it has occurred to you, but she is so very
religious, it's hardly normal. For the purposes of a story
only, of course, one might exaggerate the abnormality,
present the Controller with some unholy hidden vice
which she would discover, and then, given the right
circumstances – –'

'Religious mania?' Mr Phillips inquired doubtfully. 'I seem to have read something like it before – I never can remember the names of books, but – –'

'Of course it has been done before,' said Mr Wood with a frown. 'Everything has. That's the worst of this game. But I'm asked to propound a plot on the spur of the moment and that's the best that I can do. I'm sorry if – –'

'Oh, but Mr Phillips didn't mean that,' Mrs Hopkinson hastened to assure him. 'I think it's a lovely idea, and I'm sure we all do. And when it's written down, I'm certain nobody will ever guess the secret till the last chapter, except lucky us, who were in at the start. You *will* write it, won't you, Mr Wood?'

He shook his head.

'I'm afraid not. Even if I had the leisure for writing here, I couldn't possibly do it – put real people into a book, I mean.'

'Well, if you say not, but it does seem a shame. . . . Still, there'd be no harm in seeing how the book would go, if there was a book, so to speak? And it might always come in handy for you if you were going to write a real book later on, about something different, wouldn't it? I'm sure we'd all love to help you.'

'I don't quite follow you.'

'I think,' said Edelman in his heavy precise manner, 'that what Mrs Hopkinson has in mind is that we should beguile our leisure by constructing an imaginary detective tale, casting ourselves for the various parts – –'

'That's it, exactly!'

'With you, of course, as editor-in-chief, so to speak. It might be amusing.'

'Well, it is an idea, certainly,' Wood admitted. 'I don't know quite how – –'

'My dears, I must fly!' Mrs Hopkinson exclaimed,

gathering her belongings hastily together. 'Just look at the time! Thanks ever so for a lovely evening. I think it's a thrilling notion. We'll have a good old pow-wow about it later on. I'm sure I shall dream of horrors! Good night all!'

Her flurried departure broke up the party. Soon afterwards the other ladies went to bed, followed by Phillips and Wood. Pettigrew remained, staring into the fire, his nose wrinkled in a fashion peculiar to him when deep in thought. Then he looked across the room at Edelman and chuckled softly.

'What's the joke?' It was so rare for Edelman to put a direct question that the effect was quite startling.

'I was just thinking that you seem to have insured against Mrs Hopkinson being your partner at bridge for quite a time to come.'

Edelman uttered a short, mirthless laugh.

'That is one advantage, certainly,' he said drily. 'It will give her something else to do.'

'Quite. Let us hope there will be no compensating disadvantages.'

But his tone did not sound particularly hopeful.

# CHAPTER THREE

## The Blenkinsop File

THE late Lord Eglwyswrw's mansion was a regular two-storeyed building, disproportionately long for its breadth, perched precariously half-way down the steep slope of the north side of Marsett Bay.

The entrance faced the hill, and owing to the lie of the land, the ground floor, supported by stout rusticated columns on the seaward side, rode high above the derelict gardens running down towards the beach. Beneath it was a semi-basement, so designed that his lordship's domestic staff should have the assistance of a north light supplied through grated windows, without being distracted from their duties by any view of the bay to the south. This now stood empty. It was equipped for an air raid shelter, and would have made an admirable one, if air raids had been known at Marsett Bay.

The bedroom storey housed the voluminous records of the Pin Control. Here the weight of the accumulated files had already caused the floor to sag in one or two places and prompted the introduction of some incongrous wooden beams among the ornamental pillars of the reception rooms beneath.

It was on the ground floor that the main work of the Control was carried on. The late owner had allowed his architect to design for him a suite of long, lofty and exquisitely ugly rooms fit for entertaining half the countryside and for very little else. It was left to the Control for the first time to populate these echoing saloons. The Ministry of Works played its part in furnishing them with trestle tables and office chairs and dividing them where necessary into cubicles with partions of ply-wood and frosted glass, which reached less than half-way to the ceiling. But even so, as Mrs Hopkinson remarked, the result was not very homely.

Even Miss Clarke, important though her position was in the hierarchy of the Pin Control, did not occupy a room of her own. In this she was less fortunate than Pettigrew, but it was a misfortune that visited itself principally on her subordinates in the Licensing department. From behind the flimsy screen that secluded her from the rank and file she was able to hear everything that went on, and they knew that at any moment she was liable to pounce upon the unwary. Miss Clarke was a great pouncer.

On the morning succeeding the murderous discussion at the Fernlea Residential Club, Miss Clarke, as though to atone for the levity into which she had allowed herself to be drawn, had been at her most severe. She had pounced frequently and violently. She was in the mood, common from time to time to most capable organizers, of wanting to meddle in every detail of everybody else's work. The result was a very jumpy morning for the staff. Even Mrs Hopkinson had to run the gauntlet of her inquisition. But they by now had been long versed in Miss Clarke's ways. By dint of sheer bullying she had made them unquestionably the most efficient section in the whole office. To the public, clamouring for licences to manufacture, acquire, or dispose of pins, they appeared evasive, dilatory, and imperturbably indifferent; but administratively they were well-nigh perfect. They knew all the answers, even the answers to Miss Clarke's questions. Or so it seemed, until, in an evil hour, Miss Clarke called for the Blenkinsop file.

'Miss Danville!' Miss Clarke's leonine head appeared round the door of her cubicle. "*Miss Danville!*"

Honoria Danville, though she vainly hoped that nobody else suspected it, was in fact more than a little deaf. Also, her mind was at the moment wandering some way from her work. She had of late found it increasingly hard to concentrate on the things of this world, with the other world seeming nearer and more important every day. None the less, the second repetition of her name was loud enough to bring her back to her surroundings with a start. She rose, smoothed down her dress with fingers that trembled a little, and answered, 'Yes, Miss Clarke.'

'Will you bring me the Blenkinsop file, please, XP782.' The head withdrew.

Miss Danville looked hopelessly at the litter of papers on the table before her, and then began to search. It always took her twice as long to find a file as anybody else, a fact that Miss Clarke had learned and accepted with a certain genial contempt, but this time she began her task with a sense of despair. She was sure she would not find the file. And in this she was perfectly right. Five full minutes later she trailed down the long room into Miss Clarke's apartment, empty-handed.

Miss Clarke, without looking up from her desk, extended her hand for the file. The gesture was characteristic of her in her more unpleasant moods, and appeared to be designed to emphasize that the staff were machines serving the interests of the Pin Control, rather than human beings. But in this instance, the machine failed to function. The extended hand remained unfilled. After a pause, during which she deliberately read through the letter which she was holding in the other hand, Miss Clarke was compelled to treat Miss Danville as a human being, and a very fallible one at that.

'Well?' she said, turning towards her. 'Miss Danville, I am waiting. The Blenkinsop file, please.'

'I'm awfully sorry, Miss Clarke, but I haven't got it.'

'Not got it?' Miss Clarke's expression was one of disbelief rather than displeasure. 'But you must have it. It is marked out to you.'

'Oh yes,' Miss Danville agreed eagerly. 'It was marked out to me all right, I know. It's on my list.'

'Very well then.'

If a file is marked out to you, Miss Clarke's tone implied, you have it. That is the System of the department, and if the System errs, then chaos is come again.

'But I haven't *got* it.' Miss Danville was trembling. 'I've looked and looked and – –' Her face cleared suddenly. 'Oh – I've just remembered. Of course, Mr Edelman's got it.'

'Really, Miss Danville, this will not do. You know perfectly well that when a file is marked out to another section, the carbon transfer slip must be placed in my tray. I suppose you sent it up to Registry along with the top copy. You girls are getting too careless. Ring up Registry and ask for it back. Then – – What is the matter?'

'I – I don't think there was a transfer slip,' Miss Danville faltered.

Miss Clarke's expression, from being merely severe, became outraged.

'No transfer slip?' she echoed. Then, with the air of one determined to probe iniquity to its depths, she went on. 'Then perhaps you will tell me where is A.14's requisition note for the file?'

Even her profound emotion could not make her forget that officially Mr Edelman was A.14.

Miss Danville, quite unstrung, could only shake her head.

'No requisition note?' Miss Clarke went on remorselessly.

'No.' Miss Danville squeaked in a curious high-pitched tone. 'No. Mr Edelman just came into the room the other day, Wednesday, I think it was, or Thursday, no, Wednesday I'm almost sure, it doesn't matter which, I suppose, and said "Can I have the Blenkinsop file for a bit?" and I said, "Oh yes, I suppose so," and he put it under his arm and walked off with it, and I never thought anything about it, because I knew the file wouldn't be likely to be wanted again in a hurry, as I'd sent them a form P.C.52 only the day before, and that always keeps them quiet for *ages,* and so – – Well, that's what happened,' she concluded, her torrent of words stopping as abruptly as it had begun.

There was a shocked silence at the end of her recital. Chaos, Miss Clarke's expression indicated, had come again indeed.

'I see,' she said at last, grimly. 'Well, now that you have remembered the whereabouts of the file, perhaps you will oblige me by fetching it.'

'From Mr Edelman?' Miss Danville asked nervously.

'Obviously – unless somebody else has decided to have it for a bit, in which case you will fetch it from that person,' Miss Clarke replied with bitter irony.

'Might – might I send a messenger for it, Miss Clarke? Mr Edelman is sometimes rather – difficult.'

'That was why I suggested that you should fetch it yourself. I see no reason for adding to the messengers' difficulties. And while you are about it, please give my compliments to Mr Edelman, and draw his attention to Registry's standing order governing Transit of Files. Take this copy with you. It may assist your memory.'

A.14 was the Research section, and the Research section consisted of Mr Edelman. He was, in every sense, in a singular position. He had arrived some time after the rest of the Control, installed himself in an alcove of one of the largest rooms, where the Ministry of Works presently immured him in a plywood compartment of his own, and there he remained, all day and every day, shrouded in fumes of tobacco smoke, an object of mystery to everyone else. He had no secretary and never troubled the harassed maidens of the typing pool with demands on their services. All that was known of his activities was that into his room went a never-ending procession of files, and from it proceeded a no less continuous stream of immense hand-written minutes. The fact that gave Mr Edelman's occupation its peculiar prestige was that these minutes, as cross-questioning of the messengers revealed, went direct from A.14 to the Controller himself. What became of them thereafter, nobody knew. They did not, like the minutes of lesser men, percolate down to the Licensing section, the Enforcement branch, or the Raw Materials group. Marketing and Export, who between them had their fingers in nearly every pie baked by the Control, knew no more about them than the rest. The current gossip was that they formed part of the staple diet of the Policy Committee at its monthly meetings, and this seemed a plausible suggestion; but since the Policy Committee met in London under the chairmanship of the Minister himself, its agenda were not matters on which the rank and file could speak with any assurance.

The one thing that was obvious about Mr Edelman was that he was a glutton for work. His hours were long, although he had no superior authority to keep him up to the mark – unless the Controller, in some omniscient fashion, contrived to keep an eye on his activities. Moreover, not content with the daily ration of files which the messengers brought him – again, so it was said, direct from the Controller's sanctum itself – he had an easy-going habit of wandering through the department from time to time and requisitioning papers impartially from other sections. No worker objected to this practice – everybody had so many files in current use that the disappearance of one from the table was a positive blessing – and there was always the hope that when it returned it might prove to be enriched by one of the legendary Edelman minutes. It was a hope that had never yet been fulfilled. Naturally, the wary ones automatically safeguarded themselves by filling in at least one of the half-dozen forms that the System provided for such contingencies. It was only in the case of Miss Danville, who was in her own way as easy-going as Mr Edelman, that trouble resulted.

Miss Danville nervously picked her way between the serried tables of the Enforcement branch. Enforcement, for some reason, was exclusively male, just as Licensing was predominantly female. At the far corner of the room was Mr Edelman's door. She knocked nervously on it. There was no answer, and after standing uncertainly outside it, horribly conscious of the amused glances of the Enforcement men behind her, she screwed up her courage and went in.

The first thing that she noticed about the cubicle was that it was extremely stuffy. The Ministry of Fuel and Power's Permitted Date had passed, and consequently the whole house was kept reasonably warm by the excellent central heating inherited from Lord Eglwyswrw; but this was evidently not enough for A.14. An electric radiator at full blast filled the tiny apartment with almost unbearable heat. It served to emphasize Mr Edelman's lordly attitude to the System and all that it stood for. For even Miss Danville knew that private additions to the official heating installation were forbidden. The stuffiness was accentuated by the smoke from a short, black pipe, clenched firmly between Mr Edelman's teeth. Miss Danville coughed.

At the sound, Mr Edelman raised his head, and peered at her through horn-rimmed glasses.

'Oh it's you, is it?' he said abstractedly, laying his pipe on the table and scattering ash over the paper on which he was writing. He stared for a moment, as if he had never seen her before, and then, suddenly coming to life, said briskly, 'I know — Blenkinsop! I've done with him, thanks very much. Do you want to take him with you?'

'Yes please. And, Mr Edelman, Miss Clarke says — —'

But Mr Edelman was not paying any attention to what Miss Clarke had to say. He was kneeling behind his desk, burrowing in a mass of files that lay higgledy-piggledy on the floor. Almost immediately he found what he wanted, and rising to his feet pressed an untidy bundle of papers into her hands.

'There you are!' he said genially. 'Thanks for the memory. I'm afraid I've made rather a mess of him, but he's all there. Present, if not correct.' His earnest face lit up with a smile at his own wit.

'Oh, Mr Edelman!' Miss Danville stared in dismay at the eviscerated file in her hands.

This is not the place to describe the Control's regulations for the arrangement of files. It is enough to say that in them the System reached its apogee. One glance at the corpse of Blenkinsop was enough to establish that here every one of them had been ruthlessly violated.

'I had to pull him about a bit to get what I wanted,' Edelman said airily. 'They tie these things up in such a ridiculous way.' Then, seeing Miss Danville's look of despair, he went on in a kindly tone, 'Look here, sit down and put it straight before you go. It's no good my offering to help you, but you're welcome to my desk.'

Miss Danville shook her head miserably.

'Miss Clarke wants it at once,' she said. 'I'll have to take it as it is.'

'Oh, so the Clarke is after you, is she? My sympathies. Well, in that case – –'

He sat down at his desk again and drew his paper towards him.

'And she asked me to give you this.'

She laid the Registry's standing order on Transit of Files in front of him. Edelman contemplated it with disgust.

'Oh, this – rubbish!' he exclaimed, evidently substituting the word at the last moment for something a good deal more expressive.

'Why on earth should I have to waste my time – –' He stopped abruptly and looked closely at Miss Danville. 'I say,' he went on in a different tone, 'has the Clarke been making your life a misery over this?'

Miss Danville pursed her lips and said nothing. An odd sense of loyalty to the Licensing section, which she acknowledged to herself to be quite ridiculous, kept her silent.

'I see she has,' Edelman said quietly. He lit a spill of paper at the electric fire and applied it to his pipe. 'What a so-and-so that woman is,' he remarked between puffs. 'I wonder nobody's pushed her over the cliffs one of these dark nights. That reminds me – of course you went to bed early last night, and didn't hear all our discussion – but don't you think the Clarke would be a very suitable subject for murder? I must get Wood's views on it. I'm sure you feel like killing her sometimes, don't you?'

Really, Miss Danville was saying to herself, the heat in here is something dreadful. And the smoke – one can hardly breathe. If I don't get out of here, I shall faint, I'm sure I shall. But she did not move, and a moment later she realized that she could not move. A strange, yet familiar sensation crept through her – a feeling of divine elation that was at the same time intermingled with deep despair. Time stood still, and she felt as though she had been for untold ages shut in this airless cabin, where the tobacco smoke wreathed like incense, and the desk-lamp gleamed on Edelman's dark, satanic face, as he spoke words of death. Kill Miss Clarke. Was this then her destiny – this the meaning of the voices that she heard so often and strove so hard to interpret? The Master was speaking, and now his message was plain.

'God almighty! What's the matter with you?' exclaimed Edelman suddenly. 'What are you staring at me like that for?'

The spell was broken. 'Get thee behind me, Satan!' she cried hoarsely. 'Thou shalt not take the name of the Lord thy God in vain!' and she ran from the room.

'Well, I'll be damned!' murmured Edelman.

He rose, carefully closed the door which she had left open behind her, and plunged into his work again.

# CHAPTER FOUR

## Chivalry in the Canteen

MR WOOD worked in the Enforcement branch, at the same table as Mr Phillips, in the corner near A.14's door. He could not help hearing Miss Danville's last words, and he looked up as she brushed past him.

'Good Lord!' he said to his neighbour. 'Did you notice that?'

Mr Phillips, who was a slow and conscientious worker, looked up from his papers reluctantly.

'Notice what?' he said. 'Oh, Miss Danville – she seemed to be in rather a hurry.'

'You mean you didn't hear? My dear chap, I was right about that woman. She's crackers!'

Phillips looked at him with grave concern.

'I trust you are mistaken,' he said. 'Mental derangement is a terrible calamity for a woman – terrible.'

'Well, it's terrible for anybody, man or woman, if you come to that,' Wood replied. 'I don't mean that I'm not sorry for the poor thing, but I suggested last night that I thought she was a bit crazy and now I'm sure of it.' He reached for a scrap of paper and began to scribble notes on it. 'The only trouble from my point of view is that it makes the whole thing too easy,' he murmured.

Phillips, who usually resented interruptions to his work, seemed on this occasion quite prepared to pursue the subject.

'Too easy?' he echoed. 'Insanity, surely, doesn't make things easy. It makes them difficult – very difficult indeed.'

'Don't mean that at all,' grunted Wood between his

jottings. 'From my point of view, I said. The writer's point of view. A mad murderer explains everything. Supplies his own motive. Needn't behave in character. Can kill most improbable people. It's a piece of cake. I thought I'd explained all that yesterday.'

'Of course, of course,' Phillips agreed. 'Only, I didn't realize at the time – I mean, if Miss Danville is really – er – abnormal, doesn't it make the whole thing rather – rather dangerous?'

'I don't see that it does.' Wood carefully folded up his paper and put it away. 'She doesn't know the part we've cast her for, you see. No reason why she should. Otherwise, I agree, she might take the game seriously. No, what I was wondering was whether it would be better to have her murder Miss Clarke – that would be a bit too obvious, perhaps – or Edelman. On the whole, though, I see Edelman as a villain. Perhaps he could use her to carry out his own ends – the Svengali motive, you know. He'd enjoy that, I fancy.'

He looked at the clock. 'Quarter to one,' he observed. 'I'm going down to the canteen before it gets too crowded. Are you coming?'

'Er – not just yet. I think I'll just finish what I'm on first. Please don't wait for me.'

'I shan't.' Wood left him with a grin. It had not escaped his notice that Miss Brown usually came into lunch at a quarter past one, and that Phillips nowadays always happened to be at the entrance to the canteen just in time to meet her there. His grin was without malice. It must, he felt, be an uneasy business trying to conduct an incongruous courtship under the eyes of several hundred people.

Miss Brown, meanwhile, was standing beside Pettigrew's desk while he read through a long draft which she had just typed from his dictation. Her work, he had discovered, was neat, quick, and accurate, and it was seldom that he found very much to correct. Miss Brown, too, was well aware of her own qualities, and her expression was one of meek self-satisfaction as one sheet after another was read, approved, and laid aside. She was therefore taken entirely by surprise when Pettigrew, near the end of his perusal, suddenly burst into a shout of uncontrollable laughter.

'Is anything the matter, Mr Pettigrew?' she asked.

Pettigrew took off his spectacles, wiped them, blew his nose, and became himself once more.

'I apologize,' he said. 'But this place is so damnably dull that anything out of the way seems irresistibly funny. It's this bit here – just look at it.'

Miss Brown followed his pointing finger and read: 'The decision is hardly compatible with *Campkin v. Eager,* but that case, it should be remembered, was decided at Nicey Priors.'

'Who do you suppose the Nicey Priors were?' asked Pettigrew, beginning to chuckle again. 'They sound an amiable crowd of old gentlemen.'

'I don't know, I'm sure,' said Miss Brown, blushing uncomfortably, 'but that is what you dictated, Mr Pettigrew.' She began to turn over the leaves of her shorthand notes.

'No doubt it was. Don't bother to turn it up. It was my fault for not explaining that I was talking lawyer's Latin, and with a lawyer's false quantities at that.' He crossed out the words, wrote in 'Nisi Prius', and murmured, 'Poor old Priors! I'm quite sorry to see them go. But they had no business in the Court of Exchequer. Their proper place obviously was the Council of Nicea. Are you well up in the early Christian Fathers, Miss Brown?'

Miss Brown was not, and indicated the fact rather

shortly. But Pettigrew, chasing his own fancy, failed to see the danger sign.

'Neither am I, to be honest. I fear they are rather a neglected tribe nowadays. Miss Danville, I dare say, is quite an authority on the subject.'

Miss Brown looked her superior full in the eyes.

'I wish you wouldn't all make fun of poor Miss Danville,' she said with unwonted firmness. 'She is a very, very nice person, and it's not at all fair.'

She gathered up her papers and retreated, leaving Pettigrew for once in his life utterly at a loss for words.

But it was not what his secretary had said that had caused his confusion, although later he reflected rather bitterly that an elderly man making fun of a young woman's very natural ignorance cut a somewhat ridiculous figure and deserved any snub he might get. Her real impression on him had been made before she ever opened her mouth. He realized to his great surprise that this was the first time they had ever looked at each other directly. She had a trick of avoiding people's eyes which he had noted before. Now he was suddenly aware that Miss Brown was the possessor of a pair of large, intensely blue eyes, so vivid and brilliant as entirely to transform her otherwise unremarkable face. The discovery was quite upsetting.

'And I thought she was plain!' he told himself. 'Those eyes could be pretty dangerous used the right way.' His nose wrinkled. 'Thank heaven,' he mused, 'given proper care, there's no reason why she should ever turn them on to me again, anyway.'

He was perfectly honest with himself, but none the less, when Miss Brown, a few moments later, put her head round the door to announce that she was going to lunch, he felt irrationally disappointed that as usual she looked firmly at his feet.

Pettigrew went into lunch late. By the time he arrived in the canteen it was already emptying. He helped himself to a plate of the stew that was the staple fare at Marsett Bay and found a seat without difficulty. From where he sat he could see the Controller, blond, fattish, and a little bald, lunch *tête-à-tête* with the head of the Export Department, one of the few other permanent Civil Servants in the Control. In their neat, black suits, and with their serious, aloof expressions, they contrived to bring into their incongruous surroundings an indefinable atmosphere of Whitehall. Further down the room, he noticed two heads close together – Phillips's iron-grey hair and his secretary's mousy brown. The sight set him thinking once more of the problem that the evident state of affairs between them was likely to cause, but this time he was less concerned with its effect on himself than the possible consequences to her. He had gleaned something of her circumstances during the time that he had been at Marsett Bay, although she was not communicative and Pettigrew was the last person to wish to pry into the affairs of others. Piecing together what he had gathered, he was surprised to realize how very much alone in the world she was. She had no brothers or sisters, and her mother had apparently died several years before. Since then she had kept house for her father until his death a year or so ago. Obviously she had never made many friends of her own age, and possibly this might explain why she gravitated naturally to the society of a much older man.

What had the father been like? Pettigrew wondered, as he finished his stew, and turned to the tasteless caramel pudding that followed it. Evidently a man of some education – at least he had given a reasonably good education to his daughter, even if she didn't recognize 'Nisi Prius'. Moreover, although he found it hard to say exactly why, he had the impression that the late Mr Brown, if not a rich man, had not left his daughter entirely penniless. Miss Brown was certainly not extravagant in her dress or way of life, but Pettigrew felt distinctly that, unlike most of the typists employed by the Control, she had a 'background', and that in that background there was a modest, but assured, income.

Pettigrew frowned a little as he contemplated the picture presented by the couple at the table. On the one side, youth, inexperience, loneliness, and a bit of money; on the other side – Phillips. There was something about it that displeased him. Not that he had anything against Phillips – on the contrary, he seemed an amiable, good-natured, if rather dull, fellow. It was only in the capacity of a potential husband to Miss Brown that he disapproved of him. It was a feeling that he strove to rationalize, but not altogether to his satisfaction. He ran rapidly over in his mind what he knew of the man. An unadmitted solicitor's clerk – a snob might say that he was hardly of the same social class as Miss Brown, but that was her affair. From what he had let fall, it was to be gathered that he was a widower, and he was obviously a good twenty-five years her elder. It seemed a drab matrimonial outlook for her, but again that was a matter in which she was entitled to make her own choice. The fact that she spent her working hours in turning Pettigrew's words into odd-looking symbols on a pad of paper did not give him the right or the power to interfere. Further, Pettigrew told himself firmly, he had no desire to interfere, unless of course it should become a public duty, and there was no prospect of that. All the same. . . . Casting about for some reason to justify the dislike which he felt towards the situation, he wondered for the first time why Phillips had left his employers, at a time when solicitors' clerks were extremely scarce. He was too old, surely, to have been 'directed' into his present job. Was there some unsavoury story behind it? Quite abruptly, Pettigrew found that he was convinced that Phillips was an impostor, who had been dismissed by his employers for dishonesty, who was in fact a married man, and the sort of man that preys on young women with money. A moment later, he was laughing at himself for his melodramatic suspicions. They were, however, vivid enough for him to wish to dispose of them, and then and there he made up his mind to make a discreet inquiry from the firm where Phillips had been formerly employed. It could at least do no harm.

His train of thought was interrupted by a loud laugh, of peculiarly unpleasant quality, from a table near by. He did not need to look round to know who it came from, but he looked round none the less. Rickaby was sitting with a pretty, much made-up girl from the typing pool, whom Pettigrew had seen more than once on his occasional visits to the White Hart, Marsett Bay's principal licensed house. She too was laughing, and he wondered why she seemed so pleased with her company. For Rickaby was, of all the employees of the Control, the one whom Pettigrew disliked the most. He disliked everything about him, from his fair, slightly curly hair to his elegant pointed shoes. He disliked his vulgarity, his noisiness, the easy familiarity with which he masked without disguising his contempt for his elders. In a word (which he had coined specially for the occasion) he disliked his unsnubbability.

Pettigrew was too much of a realist not to have wondered more than once whether the root of his dislike was not the fact that Rickaby was by many years his junior, and enjoyed life, after his fashion, to a degree not given to a middle-aged bachelor in war-time. But he had been strengthened in his antipathy when he found that it was shared by most of his fellow residents at Fernlea, and that Wood, who had had to work with him at one time, complained of his incurable idleness. Above all, he had been delighted to observe that Miss Brown, at whom Rickaby had, in his own phrase, made a pass, had quietly but firmly rejected him. His confidence in her judgement in this matter was not quite in keeping with his doubts where Phillips was concerned, but even middle-aged bachelors cannot be realists all the time.

Meanwhile, Rickaby was evidently enjoying his joke, and so also was his companion. It appeared from his gestures and elaborate mouthings that he was giving an imitation of somebody. Then, in mid career of his impersonation, something occurred to interrupt him. He glanced over his shoulder towards the door, dug his neighbour violently in the ribs and at the same time assumed an air of exaggerated solemnity. This, as was to be expected, had the effect of extracting from her another peal of laughter, which she vainly tried to suppress by stuffing a handkerchief into her mouth.

Pettigrew, following Rickaby's eyes, saw Miss Danville coming down the middle of the room. He did not find anything in the spectacle in the least laughable. The poor woman was obviously distraught. She had been crying, and seemed hardly to know what she was doing. With shaking hands she endeavoured to help herself at the serving table, but only succeeded in dropping a plate. She stared at it stupidly as it lay on the floor, making no attempt to pick it up.

To Pettigrew's fury, this only caused further bursts of merriment from Rickaby's table. He half rose in his seat, undecided what to do. Before he could make up his mind, however, Miss Brown had intervened. Taking in the situation with a quickness that won Pettigrew's approval, she hurried across the room, put her arm round Miss Danville and led her to her own table. Leaving her there for a moment, she was back again almost at once with a cup of coffee and some sandwiches. Then, sitting down beside her, she began what was evidently a successful attempt to calm her. Phillips, his broad, good-natured face expressing the keenest sympathy, joined in the quiet conversation, and by the time Pettigrew left the canteen, Miss Danville appeared to be restored to tranquillity.

Miss Brown did not appear in Pettigrew's room till a quarter of an hour later.

'I am sorry I was so long over my lunch,' she said. 'But something happened to delay me.'

'You needn't apologize,' he replied. 'I saw what happened, and, if you will allow me to say so, I think you behaved very well.'

'Thank you, Mr Pettigrew.'

'If anybody ought to apologize,' Pettigrew went on, 'I think that I should. I ought not to have tried to be funny at Miss Danville's expense. It was in very bad taste. Please forget it.'

Miss Brown once more gave him the benefit of her brilliant blue eyes.

'Of course,' she murmured. 'I've brought you the draft amendments to the new Regulation, Mr Pettigrew. Do you want to go through them now?'

'That will be delightful,' Pettigrew said meekly.

Delightful or not, the draft amendments claimed his attention to the exclusion of everything else for the next two hours. At the end of that time, an ear-piercing whistle was heard outside his room. It continued for half a minute or so, and then hurried footsteps were heard in the corridor and the noise ceased abruptly.

'What on earth was that terrible din?' he asked Miss Brown, when she brought in his tea shortly afterwards.

'Miss Danville's new kettle. I'm afraid it sounds rather loud in here, but of course the gas-ring is only just next door.'

'So I had observed. But why should Miss Danville's new kettle be of this peculiarly strident type?'

'I do hope you won't find it too disturbing, Mr Pettigrew, but it was my idea, really. You see, Miss Danville makes the tea for all this side of the building – that reminds me, she asked me to collect one and eightpence from you for this month – and last week she let a kettle burn right through because she forgot all about it. You know, she is rather apt to forget things sometimes,' she added in the tone of one deprecating the shortcomings of a much loved pet dog.

'That also I had noticed, but I am glad she doesn't forget to collect her dues. Here's your one and eightpence. Then the musical kettle is intended as a gentle reminder of her duties? In principle it seems an excellent idea, but need it be quite so loud?'

'Well,' said Miss Brown as though she were confessing to a weakness of her own, 'the fact is, Miss Danville is just a little deaf. You won't tell anyone, will you? I don't think she would like it to be known. So when I bought the kettle, naturally I got the loudest one I could find. But of course, if you object, Mr Pettigrew – –'

'Object? When my afternoon tea and Miss Danville's peace of mind are at stake? Certainly not. I shall look forward to it every day with eagerness. By the way, are these kettles expensive things? Because if so, you must let me contribute – –'

'I couldn't think of it, Mr Pettigrew. Have you finished with your tray?'

# CHAPTER FIVE

## Encounter at 'The Gamecock'

LOOKING back afterwards, Pettigrew dated from these events the beginning of a new and decidedly less agreeable period in his life at the Control, particularly so far as the part of it that was spent at Fernlea was concerned. The atmosphere at the Residential Club, he found, had changed entirely. Its inhabitants, instead of being a collection of individuals trying, more or less successfully, to tolerate one another's peculiarities, showed now an ever increasing tendency to divide themselves into two sharply opposed groups. The fact that there was only one sitting-room in which to spend the lengthening winter evenings made the split all the more apparent.

The dividing line between the two parties was their attitude towards the criminal fantasy in process of being devised by Wood – 'the Plot', as it was called by its adepts; and the fact that determined to which party any individual should belong was soon seen to be a purely personal one – his or her attitude to Miss Danville. She had made it clear from the start that she disapproved of the whole business, and the fact that she had been cast for the crucial role in it without her knowledge had the effect of transforming what had been begun as an amusing parlour game into a kind of conspiracy from which she had to be vigorously excluded. Used as she was to living in a world of her own, she would probably not have resented being left in a minority of one, even if she had noticed it. But Miss Brown, who had now assumed the function of protector towards her, saw to it that she was not. Under her influence, Phillips too deserted the ranks of the plotters and the trio formed a solid group every evening in one corner of the room, while the opposition party occupied another.

The leader of the plotters was, of course, Wood, who was now never without a sheaf of notes from which he would regale his admirers with the latest ideas that had occurred to him during the day. Edelman was a powerful supporter – a trifle too powerful for the author's taste, sometimes, when his fertile imagination threatened to take charge of the plot altogether, or, as Wood put it, 'upset the whole balance of the story'. Miss Clarke, too, had now come out wholeheartedly in its favour. Her previous objections were outweighed by the prospect of putting Miss Danville in a ridiculous light, and she was prepared even to co-operate with Edelman, against whom, inside the office, she was still waging an endless war of memoranda regarding the condition of the Blenkinsop file. Mrs Hopkinson, now a more frequent visitor than ever, was of little practical assistance but was a noisy and uncritical admirer of everything that anybody else thought of. Finally, even Rickaby was initiated into the scheme, less because he had become any more popular with the others than because it was obviously impossible for him to belong to the opposition.

To Pettigrew, hovering uneasily between the two parties and striving to keep on good terms with both, it was a somewhat disquieting situation. For one thing, his orderly, legal mind was offended by the fact that the plotters seemed to have no notion of what they proposed to do with the plot which they were perpetually discussing, altering, and elaborating. Wood, indeed, evidently had the vague idea that at some future date it might, when suitably disguised, form the foundation for a publishable novel; and this was at least reasonable. Mrs Hopkinson more than once made the wholly impracticable suggestion that the thing should be somehow transmogrified into an entertainment which could be acted for the amusement of the staff at Christmas. (She caused some amusement to the others when she offered to dye her hair in order to play one of the parts more effectively.) But for the rest, they appeared to be content with the exercise of their imaginations on a theme that grew steadily more and more fantastic.

It was, he concluded, the effect of the situation in which they found themselves. None of them had any interests in Marsett Bay outside their work. Many of the married employees had managed to transfer their families to the neighbourhood and so to maintain a more or less normal existence out of office hours. But except for Edelman, whose wife and child were in America, the Fernlea residents were unmarried. Time hung heavy on their hands, and it was natural that they should employ it in some way. But he wished devoutly that they could have hit upon some other. It was, he felt obscurely, decidedly unhealthy. More particularly, he could not believe that Miss Danville could be kept indefinitely in ignorance of the part assigned to her in what Mrs Hopkinson had inevitably christened 'the Perfect Crime'. And from what he knew of her, he feared that the disclosure when it came might have a serious effect upon her. He ventured to mention this consideration to Edelman, whom he judged to be the most reasonable member of his set. The result was disappointing. Edelman listened to him gravely, and remarked in a dispassionate tone that he was probably right, and that although it was impossible to predict human reactions with any real accuracy, the results would certainly be of interest. Pettigrew felt as though he was listening to a chemist discussing the possible outcome of an experiment. He did not pursue the subject any further.

On the day of this conversation, Pettigrew received a letter which served to relieve him of at least one of his anxieties. It came from his tenant in the Temple.

'Dear Frank,' it ran. 'Many thanks for your letter. I have made the inquiries you asked for. As I expected, old Tillotson professed to be shocked at my demand, which he quite properly regarded as an attempt to induce a breach of professional confidence. As I also expected, he ended by coming across with what I wanted. I enclose a copy of his letter. It all seems quite satisfactory, though the gentleman must be getting a bit long in the tooth for a second marriage, to judge by the dates.

'Three circuit briefs have come my way recently, marked "for Mr Pettigrew, on war service." The half fees will be duly paid into your account, as we arranged. I was at Rampleford Assizes last week. Your absence was much deplored, but the mess is only a shadow of itself these days. Yours ever, Bill.'

The enclosure was in the following terms:

'Your friend need not be in any doubt that Mr Phillips is in fact a widower – unless he has re-married, as to which, I have, of course, no information. My firm acted for him in securing probate of the late Mrs Sarah Emily Phillips's will as long ago as 1931. On turning up the papers, I see that she actually died on the 19th September in that year at Bloomington Hospital, Herts, her husband being the sole executor. I think that this information should serve his purpose, and he will, I know, treat it as strictly confidential.

'Perhaps I should add that Mr Phillips entered the firm's employment in 1919, and while with us gave complete satisfaction. The particular branch of our activities with which he was concerned came to a standstill on the declaration of war, and although we should have been glad to employ him in another capacity at a not very reduced salary, he expressed a desire to find work elsewhere more closely associated with the war effort. We should certainly be prepared to consider his re-employment on the cessation of hostilities, should an opening then exist. I should point out, to avoid any possible misunderstanding, that the statutory provisions governing Reinstatement in Civil Employment do not apply in his case.'

Nothing, Pettigrew told himself, could be more satisfactory. And if, at the same time, he felt a wholly illogical twinge of disappointment, that was clearly attributable to the craving for melodrama that clings even to mature men engaged in the most humdrum occupations. Henceforward, he could watch the development of the romance with disinterested eyes. Provided, of course, that it did not interfere with Miss Brown's work – and so far there was no sign of that.

In the course of the next week or so he realized that there were other eyes on the situation which were not quite so disinterested. Mrs Hopkinson began to manifest unmistakable signs of dislike for Phillips. Hitherto, there had never, so far as Pettigrew's observation went, been anything 'between' them, either by way of affection or the reverse. But, as Phillips grew progressively more and more engrossed with Miss Brown, the Merry Widow became steadily sourer towards him. At the same time, after her proposal for a dramatic version of the Plot had been rejected for the last time, her interest in it abruptly fell off. By way of compensation, apparently, she decided to devote her energies to 'taking up', or alternatively 'bringing out' Miss Brown, in whom she had always shown a rather embarrassing maternal interest. And to this operation Phillips was an obvious and annoying obstacle. The alliance between Miss Brown and Miss Danville, whom she openly despised, naturally added to her ill humour.

To his dismay, Pettigrew found himself, not for the first time, the recipient of unwanted confidences. Penning him in a corner of the room, Mrs Hopkinson bewailed to him that the girl was getting into the wrong hands. Something, she insisted vaguely, should be done about it. Did Pettigrew know that she had three hundred a year of her own? Pettigrew did not, and wondered very much whether Mrs Hopkinson did, or whether she had invented the figure as a likely one. Three hundred a year! she repeated, nodding her copper curls, and no boy friends! It wasn't natural, at that age, was it? As to Phillips, it was obvious that he was a fortune-hunter. There was only his word for it that he was a widower at all. Ten to one he had a wife and half a dozen kids somewhere. She knew that sort. It made her downright sick to see him getting away with it, and that old looney of a Danville egging her on all the time. A young thing like that ought to be enjoying herself and seeing life, the same as she had when she was a girl, instead of tying herself up with a man old enough to be her father. *She* knew, Mrs Hopkinson concluded reminiscently, what it was to make a mistake of that kind, and it wasn't everybody who was as lucky as she had been, either.

Pettigrew, left to conclude that Mrs Hopkinson's luck had consisted in Mr Hopkinson deciding to die conveniently early, contented himself with inarticulate murmurs and managed to avoid committing himself. Privately, he felt bound to admit that the Merry Widow's views, though differently expressed, were not so very far from those which he had himself felt only a short time before. He did not feel at liberty to set her mind at rest regarding Phillips's widowerhood, and when pressed further for his opinion in the matter, evaded the issue by pointing out that Miss Brown had not tied herself up yet.

Indeed, it was singularly difficult to say as yet whether Miss Brown did in fact propose to tie herself up with Phillips or not. His intentions were obvious. So was Miss Danville's enthusiastic support of his suit. No match-making mother ever encouraged a man more. Mrs Hopkinson, never given to finesse, could not have made her disapproval plainer. Miss Brown remained the sole unknown quantity. Always calm and quiet, she appeared equally serene and contented whether she was by herself, with Phillips, with Miss Danville, or, as more often happened, in the company of the two together. She even seemed to tolerate Mrs Hopkinson, though that lady complained bitterly that she 'could get nothing out of her'. Her self-possession, Pettigrew felt, was admirable. He began to wonder whether she was not better able to look after herself than he had supposed.

One evening, Pettigrew felt that he could stand the atmosphere of the Fernlea no longer. He had had a tiring day. The Controller had been exceptionally obstructive over the amendments by which Pettigrew had hoped to introduce some semblance of logic into the wild ramifications of the latest Order governing the marketing of pins. Miss Danville had neglected to make the tea until her whistling kettle had blown its piercing blast for five agonizing minutes. The war news was depressing. And now the evening session in the lounge was in full swing. The plotters were huddled in their corner, eagerly discussing some new absurdity introduced by Edelman. From time to time their colloquy was interrupted by bursts of laughter, interspersed with meaning glances in the direction of Miss Danville and no less meaning cries of 'Sh-h!' Miss Danville, her lips moving slowly, was absorbed in her book, from which she raised her eyes occasionally to cast approving glances at Miss Brown and Phillips, sitting together on the sofa, speaking little but apparently satisfied in each other's company. When the door opened to admit Mrs Hopkinson, Pettigrew decided on action. Side-stepping her neatly, he slipped into the hall, took his hat and coat off the peg, and walked out of the house.

'What I need,' he said to himself as he groped his way along the pavement, 'is a drink.' It came to him with surprise that it was a long time since he had had one. There was something monastic about the atmosphere of Marsett Bay that seemed to inhibit his thirst. Perhaps it was because he had so far not found anybody there he particularly wanted to drink with. Whatever the reason, he felt that by now it was decidedly overdue.

At the corner of the High Street, he hesitated. Just across the way was the White Hart. It would be, he knew, crowded with the bright young things of the Control, and in his present mood he did not want to see any more of his fellow government servants. The Crown, farther down the road, would not be much better. Where else was there? He remembered that down an alley-way somewhere on his left he had noticed a little pub bearing the sign of the Gamecock. (Was cock-fighting still practised in these parts, he wondered?) It occurred to him that this might be worth trying, if he could find it in the black-out. A quiet local, with its own faithful clientele, the kind of place where a casual visitor would be left severely alone, regarded with suspicion by the regulars. In his present mood, that was exactly what Pettigrew wanted.

Ten minutes later, he was sitting in a corner of a dimly lit bar parlour, absorbing a pint of weak war-time beer and thankfully reflecting that there was nobody within sight who took the smallest interest in him or was in the least likely to throw a word in his direction. He was about half-way through his tankard when he became aware that the light had suddenly become noticeably dimmer. Looking up, he found that he was in the shadow of a very tall, very broad figure that was advancing towards him from the bar. He registered the fact without any particular interest and was just putting his can to his lips again when a voice said, 'Fancy meeting you here, Mr Pettigrew!'

'Hell!' said Pettigrew under his breath as he reluctantly lowered his drink. Was he never to escape from the Control? Neither the voice nor the figure, however, seemed to belong to any of his Marsett Bay acquaintances, though both were vaguely familiar. Then the light caught the pointed tip of a long dark moustache, and he exclaimed with pleasure as well as surprise, 'Inspector Mallett, of all people! What on earth are you doing here?'

Mallett did not reply to the question at once. Instead, he produced from somewhere under his left armpit a small, wiry man with a very long nose, and said, 'This is Detective-Inspector Jellaby, of the County Constabulary, sir. We'll come and sit by you, if you've no objection.'

'Objection? Of course not!' said Pettigrew, who a moment before had been rejoicing in his solitude. His acquaintance with Inspector Mallett, of New Scotland Yard, was confined to a brief and tragic episode in his life, but he had then formed a great admiration for the beefy man with a nimble brain and he was unaffectedly pleased to see him again.

'This is the last place I expected to meet you,' he went on, when they were all settled. 'Either my reading of the newspapers has been deplorably lax, or there has been no crime of note in this part of the world. Don't tell me that there is really a plot to murder the Pin Controller.'

'*Really* a plot to murder Mr Palafox?' Mallett repeated with the innocent gravity with which he always received the most unlikely propositions. 'I can't say that I have heard of any such thing. You haven't come across anything, I hope, sir, that makes you suspect – –'

'No, no, of course not. I was only talking nonsense. It's a habit that's sadly catching in this place, I'm afraid. I have the misfortune to share lodgings with a writer of detective stories, which is rather unsettling to the imagination.'

'Quite so, sir. No, I haven't come on anything of that kind. I've been taken off my usual work at the Yard to – to poke my nose into matters up here generally.'

'I see. I had no idea that the Control could be an object of interest to Scotland Yard.'

'I don't think I mentioned the Control, Mr Pettigrew,' said Mallett cautiously.

'But you did mention the name of the Controller, and I'm hanged if I can see why you should bother to find that out unless – –'

The end of the sentence was drowned in a rumble of genial laughter from Mallett.

'You had me there, sir,' he confessed. 'I ought to have known better. You must let me order you another pint for that.'

'I suppose,' said Pettigrew, when the fresh drinks had been brought, 'you can't tell me what the affairs you are interested in amount to?'

He was conscious that Inspector Jellaby was looking down his long nose in a disapproving manner, but Mallett did not seem disturbed by the question. He took a long drink, carefully wiped his moustaches, and appeared to meditate before he replied.

'Your position here, sir, is that of legal adviser to the Control?'

'Quite right.'

'And you have, of course, no connexion, past or present, with the trade?'

'The pin trade? I don't know the first thing about it.'

'Exactly. I don't know if you realize, Mr Pettigrew, quite how singular you are in that respect, so far as the Control is concerned.'

'Am I? I'm afraid I never gave any great thought to the matter. Naturally, I took it for granted that it was largely staffed by experts. It's not my pigeon, really.'

'Just so. And the experts, of course, are drawn from the trade. Above a certain level, the great majority of the workers here are in peace-time employed by the firms who have to be governed in war by the Control. It's inevitable, really. They are the only people who could do the job.'

'I am lamentably incurious about my fellows except where they concern me personally,' said Pettigrew. 'I don't talk shop with them or they with me. I don't even know how most of the people I see every day earn their livings in civil life.'

'You stay at the Fernlea Residential Club, don't you?' the inspector said. 'Let me see . . . Edelman is advertisement manager to a big marketing company. Wood was head clerk to another firm in the same line. Rickaby is the nephew of the chairman of the largest exporters of pins in the world. Miss Clarke doesn't seem to have any connexion with the trade, so far as I can tell at present, but I'm not sure. Miss Brown is, of course, quite independent. That's the lot, I think.'

'Phillips,' murmured Jellaby.

'That's one man I do know about,' said Pettigrew. 'He's a solicitor's clerk.'

'Of course,' Mallett agreed. 'What was it I was telling you about his firm, Mr Jellaby?'

'Amalgamation,' Jellaby observed.

'That was it. They carried through the merger of two rival trade associations just before the war. I don't say that that is how Phillips comes to be here, but it seems likely.'

Pettigrew laughed.

'I was just thinking,' he said by way of explanation, 'that you need hardly have bothered to ask me whether I had any links with the trade. You must have known the answer before you put the question.'

'Quite so, sir,' said Mallett gravely.

'Well, Inspector, to continue – –'

'Well, to put it shortly, some of these people may find themselves in a position where their public duty and their private interest don't entirely coincide. You follow me, sir?'

'Alas for human nature, I do!'

'Ninety-nine out of a hundred of them are perfectly honest, I have no doubt. But there is always the chance of the hundredth.'

'You are not telling me, Inspector, that you came all the way to this singularly uncomfortable spot on a chance.'

'It is a bit more definite than that,' Mallett admitted. 'There have been certain things – leakages of information, breaches of the control, and so forth that made us think that a look around here would be advisable. I can't put it higher than that.'

'And I should be the last person to ask you to do so. Well, Inspector, you have at least given me a new interest in life at Marsett Bay, and for that alone I am very deeply in your debt. It's time I was getting back. There is a look in the landlord's eye that tells me he is about to call time. The worst of having police in the place is that it makes these fellows so confoundedly punctual. Good night. I don't suppose I can be of any conceivable use to you, but if I should happen to run across anything in your line, I'll let you know.'

'I shall be much obliged, sir. The police station here will always find me. Good night, sir. Oh, by the way — —'

'Yes?'

'What you said just now about a plot to murder the Controller. That was only a joke, I suppose, sir?'

'Sorry as I am to disappoint you, it was. And a very poor joke too, I'm afraid. Good night.'

# CHAPTER SIX

## A Question of Insurance

MALLETT'S presence at Marsett Bay and the matters that had brought him there did, as Pettigrew had said, add a new interest to his life at the Control, but for the next ten days after the encounter at the Gamecock he had little leisure to reflect upon it. A sudden spate of work descended on the legal adviser, which necessitated long and ever longer hours at the office, culminating in a flying visit to London where the question of the new amendments was threshed out at what in political circles are know as 'the highest levels'. During this period he caught an occasional glimpse of Mallett in the streets of the town and once in the Controller's office, which he happened to be entering just as the inspector was leaving. At all these encounters Mallett passed him by with no more than the slightest nod of recognition. Pettigrew understood without being told that he did not desire to have any undue attention called to himself in public. On his side, in spite of his vague promise of assistance, Pettigrew had no particular wish to interest himself in whatever skulduggery the inspector was investigating, even if he had the time to do so. It would certainly be dull and probably tiresome, he reflected. 'Not my pigeon,' he repeated thankfully to himself, and plunged to work again.

At last, little by little, the pressure eased. The files of papers began to dwindle, swollen no longer by the reinforcements that for days past had overflowed his 'In' tray. The telephone remained silent for hours together. Soon he was able to look across his desk to where Miss

Brown, rather pale but unshaken by the crisis, patiently took down his interminable memoranda. Then a day came when, quite suddenly, it seemed, there was nothing left to do. The last draft was approved, the last letter signed, the last minute added to the last file. And Miss Brown, conscientious to the last, was positively saying, 'Is there anything else you want me to do today, Mr Pettigrew?'

Pettigrew yawned, stretched himself, and cast incredulous eyes at his empty tray.

'Nothing,' he said. 'Absolutely nothing. There are moments when I feel that "nothing" is the most beautiful word in the language, and this is certainly one of them. There's at least an hour to go before we can decently leave the office, and it looks like being one hour of complete and blessed idleness. I suppose, being young and strong, you have some knitting in your bag to occupy you. Personally, I propose to spend the time in meditation on the beauty of nothingness. Will you be good enough to wake me up at, say, half-past five?'

Pettigrew became aware that Miss Brown had not paid the least attention to what he had been saying. She was looking at her feet, clutching her writing pad firmly in one hand, and there was a slight flush on her cheeks.

'Is anything the matter?' he asked.

She lifted her head and her brilliant blue eyes looked straight into his.

'Do you mind if I ask you something, Mr Pettigrew?'

'No, of course not. Fire ahead.'

The question, when it came, surprised him.

'Do you know anything about insurance, Mr Pettigrew?'

'Insurance? Well, I suppose so, although I'm no expert. But what kind of insurance do you mean? Fire, accident, marine, employer's liability?'

'I meant, insuring one's life. Do you think it's a good thing to do?'

'A very sensible, prudent thing to do, if one has any dependents to consider. Of course, it's impossible to advise unless one knows all the circumstances, but I should hardly have thought that you – I mean, I don't want to pry into your personal affairs, but – –'

Miss Brown's gaze had wandered down to her shoes again.

'I have a little money of my own,' she murmured. 'I could afford the premium quite well for, say, a thousand pounds. I've got some papers here which the company sent me, if you wouldn't mind looking at them.'

'Certainly I will, if you wish. But that wasn't exactly what I had in mind. I meant, a single woman doesn't usually – –' He found it strangely difficult to put it into words. 'Are you – are you proposing to get married, Miss Brown?'

Completely calm, Miss Brown replied, 'I'm not quite sure yet, but I think I am.'

Really, Pettigrew thought, this young woman is uncannily matter-of-fact. It's not natural.

'I should have thought,' he said in a tone which he could not prevent sounding a little peevish, 'that it was rather more important to decide whether to get married than whether to get insured. Aren't you putting the cart before the horse?'

Miss Brown smiled cheerfully. 'I suppose I am, really,' she said. 'Only the two things seem to hang together, somehow, and I thought you could give me some advice about insurance – –'

'Whereas my advice on the other matter would not be worth listening to? I expect you are perfectly right there.'

'Oh, I didn't mean that!'

'None the less, you had a perfect right to mean it. It would be an impertinence on my part to give an opinion where it was not asked for. But since we have gone so far, perhaps you wouldn't mind telling me who it is you are thinking of marrying. Should I be right in guessing that it was Mr Phillips?'

'Yes.'

'I needn't ask if he wants to marry you. Any doubt in the matter comes from your side.'

'Yes.'

'Well,' Pettigrew went on, beginning to be anxious to bring this embarrassing colloquy to an end, 'you will have to make up your own mind whether or not you love him.'

'Oh, but I know I don't love him,' Miss Brown replied as calmly as ever.

'Then why on earth – – ?'

'It's rather difficult to explain, really,' she said, sitting down and regarding her writing pad as though to get inspiration from it. 'You see, ever since father died I've been alone, and I'm not used to it. And I'm not at all good with young men, at least the only young men I've met. And Mr Phillips is very kind and – and sensible about things, and I know I could make him happy. I think it would be quite a good plan, really. Honoria – Miss Danville thinks so too.'

'Miss Danville!'

Miss Brown nodded. 'She's very keen on it,' she added.

'But my dear girl, you're surely not going to tell me that you are depending on Miss Danville's advice in a matter of this kind?' Remembering what had occurred the last time Miss Danville's name had come up between them, he hastened to add, 'I don't mean that I have anything against her, of course, please don't think that. But surely, a woman who has never even been married herself – –'

'That's just it,' was the reply. 'She knows what it is not to be married. I don't want to grow up to be like Miss Danville.'

Pettigrew passed his hands through his hair in despair.

'Of all the arguments for matrimony!' he groaned. 'Anyway, why should you grow up to be like Miss Danville? You might equally well turn into something like Miss Clarke.'

'Do you think that would be any better?' she retorted, and their joint laughter relieved the tension.

'By the way,' Pettigrew observed a moment later, 'was it on Miss Danville's advice that you thought of insuring your life?'

'Oh, no. That was Mr Phillips's idea, entirely.'

'I see. . . . Before you had even accepted him?'

'I'm afraid I rather let him take things for granted,' she replied demurely.

Pettigrew made no reply. His nose wrinkled in thought, he was idly drawing circles on his blotter. After a pause, Miss Brown got up.

'You haven't told me yet,' she said reproachfully, 'what you think about my insuring myself.'

'Haven't I? We seem to have discussed so many things that I quite forgot where we began. Well, I'll look through these papers of yours and tell you what I think about them. As for the question of principle, I absolutely decline to say anything until you and Miss Danville have settled your matrimonial future between you.'

'Very good, Mr Pettigrew.'

The remainder of the hour's idleness was spent in meditations rather less peaceful than those that Pettigrew had promised himself.

'This is nothing to do with me,' he told himself again and again. 'Absolutely nothing. If this young woman chooses to make a fool of herself, it is her affair, exclusively and entirely. Merely because she happens to be thrown in my way, I absolutely refuse to let myself be jockeyed into the position of father confessor.'

Nobody, it occurred to him at this point, had asked him to act as father confessor – least of all Miss Brown herself. She preferred the counsel of Miss Danville – a fact that simultaneously amused and irritated him. All she had asked him to do was to look at a proposal form for a policy of insurance. Well, why not do just that? It was a perfectly sound company, and it would take him just five minutes to glance through it and assure her that it was all in order. After that, he had no further concern in the matter. The obvious, practical, commonsense thing to do then was to wash his hands of the whole affair, let her insure her life – a prudent action, had he not just told her? – marry Phillips, and – –'

And what, exactly? Live happily ever after? He was not concerned in his secretary's happiness. Pettigrew tried to bring himself to face the problem like a rider forcing a balking horse to face an ugly fence. It wasn't a question of her living happily, it was a question, purely and simply, of her living at all. All his former suspicions of Phillips returned to him with a rush. He was a widower all right, he had established that, but what sort of a widower? A widower who had inherited some property from his wife, and who, when he thought of marrying again, looked round for a young girl, also with property of her own, entirely alone, and, as a first step towards matrimony, suggested that she should insure her life for a thousand pounds! Nobody with any knowledge of the world could fail to see the possible implications of such a situation. Could anybody, seeing them, be content to stand by and do nothing?

'Hell!' Pettigrew exclaimed aloud. This was precisely

the set of circumstances that he would instinctively seek
to avoid, with which he felt utterly incompetent to deal.
All his working life had been spent in resolving other
people's problems, but they had been the problems of
strangers, dealt with at arm's length through the
medium of a solicitor, and considered in the quiet, dust-
laden atmosphere of the Temple, where matters of life
and death, fortune and bankruptcy resolved themselves
into carefully phrased opinions and the comparison of
reported cases. It had not taught him what to do when
he found himself confronted with a girl walking blind-
fold into what might be mortal danger. He felt deeply
aggrieved that fate should have set a burden on his
shoulders, but he saw now that he could no longer
simply pretend that the burden wasn't there.

He considered, and dismissed, the idea of speaking to
Inspector Mallett. It would be a waste of time, he reflected, at this stage to consult the police with so little
to go upon. After all, it was no crime to want to marry
a woman much younger than yourself, and if you chose
to suggest to her that she should take out a policy of
insurance on her life, what affair was that of Scotland
Yard's? If there were any evidence of the first Mrs
Phillips having died anything but a natural death, why
should not Mallett, who had obviously made a close
study of the antecedents of all the Control's employees,
have mentioned it? That did not conclude the matter,
of course. How many women had George Joseph Smith
married before anyone became suspicious of all his bath-
room misadventures? Once put upon inquiry, though,
it wasn't so difficult to reveal the whole damning series
of deaths. If he could prove that Phillips's first marriage
bore a suspicious likeness to the one he was now proposing, there would at least be a case worth propounding
to Mallett.

He sat for a few moments, his nose wrinkled completely out of shape, then seized his pen and dashed off a letter to his old chambers in the Temple.

Dear Bill, I am sorry to bother you again, but please treat this as urgent. Ask no questions, and don't think me mad, but just do as I say. Ascertain as soon as you can (*a*) how much the late Mrs Phillips left; (*b*) whether her husband was sole beneficiary; (*c*) how much of the estate was represented by an insurance policy, and (*d*) – this is important – when the policy was taken out. I don't care how you find this out, whether by blackmailing old Tillotson, or by going to Somerset House (if that's where they keep wills in war-time) but I *must know*. The policy will probably have been with Empyrean, if that's any help to you.

Yours urgently,<br>FRANK

P.S. This is *not* a joke.

He had written the address and was just sealing the envelope when Miss Brown knocked at his door.

'It is half-past five, Mr Pettigrew,' she said. Then, almost coyly, she added, 'How were the meditations?'

'Very enlightening,' Pettigrew replied grimly.

# CHAPTER SEVEN

## *Answer to a Letter*

PETTIGREW only had to wait a week for the answer to his letter. He found it a very slow and anxious week to live through, and before it was over had become illogically impatient with his correspondent for the delay. Although his reason told him that Miss Brown must be perfectly safe until she was both insured and married to Phillips, the spectacle of the two lunching together in the canteen, or sitting side by side on the sofa in the Fernlea's lounge, filled him with the deepest disquiet. Not usually given to showing his feelings, he was appalled one evening to overhear a murmur from Rickaby, 'I do believe the old chap's getting jealous!' which told him that his anxiety had been observed and misconstrued. The monstrous accusation drove him out two nights running to the Gamecock, where, not meeting Mallett, he drank rather more beer than was good for him.

So far as the question of insurance was concerned, he found a simple way of playing for time. He merely told Miss Brown that the terms offered by the Empyrean were perfectly fair and reasonable, but that before deciding in the matter it would be as well as to compare them with those of some other companies – the Galaxy, for example, or the Sidereal. Miss Brown accepted his advice and said that she would get particulars from the Empyrean's rivals. The matter was thus shelved for the time being.

Pettigrew felt that he had at least put a spoke in the enemy's wheel; but if so, the enemy did not appear to notice it. Phillips remained throughout as agreeable and civil as ever, as friendly as was consistent with the difference, freely admitted and indeed insisted on by him, between a mere solicitor's clerk and a gentleman of the bar. At the same time, he continued to be quite non-committal. Neither to Pettigrew nor to anybody else did he ever mention the name of Miss Brown nor the subject of life insurance. The same sang-froid which enabled him to carry on his courtship in the most difficult and public conditions imaginable seemed also to have made him indifferent to the dark suspicions with which he was regarded. And yet, Pettigrew reflected, he must know that the girl has consulted me about the insurance. Knowing what he knows, he must surely guess what my reactions to that would be. Or does he take me for a complete fool? Then he remembered that at the heart of almost every murderer there is to be found a deep-seated vanity than blinds him to the risks he runs and so often leads to his undoing – after the event. Contemplating the amiable, affable Mr Phillips, he became gloomier than ever.

Then the looked-for letter arrived. It was short and to the point.

Dear Frank, I have done your commission, though I'm hanged if I can find any duties of this sort included in the covenants of my tenancy of the chambers. The answers to your questions are: (a) £2,347 10s. 8d. (b) Yes. (c) No policy moneys are included in the estate, which consisted of stock exchange securities, cash at bank, and the usual small trimmings. (d) Consequently does not arise. I hope you are satisfied.

By the way, you told me to ask no questions and I'm not doing so. All the same, I couldn't help wondering whether your inquiry was not the result of reading one of the gory romances of your colleague who calls himself Amyas Leigh.

Just in case this should be so, I ought to tell you that I have ascertained from Tillotson that the lady had been for three years before her death in the same hospital where she is recorded to have died. I fear, therefore that any notions you may have cherished of establishing a sudden and violent end for her must be laid aside.

Yours ever,

BILL

P.S. Just to rub it in, I have even now, through devious means which I will not divulge, ascertained that there was a policy with the Empyrean on Mrs Phillips's life for the modest sum of five hundred pounds. It was allowed to lapse, for non-payment of premiums! Are you quite happy now?

So that was that! For the second time in the space of a few weeks Pettigrew saw himself self-convicted of shameful, puerile credulity. Once more he felt the sense of anti-climax that goes with relief from the apprehension of danger. Phillips, it was now evident, was no more than a perfectly ordinary, respectable widower, bent on making a perfectly ordinary, respectable remarriage. Miss Brown's future was as safe as the earning capacity of a solicitor's clerk and a small private income could make it. No doubt she would (in a perfectly ordinary, respectable way) be extremely happy. The load of responsibility which he had shouldered so unwillingly was removed. Nothing could be more satisfactory.

If telling himself that he was relieved and pleased at finding himself mistaken could have made him look so, Pettigrew should have gone about with a positively radiant face. But for some reason which he was quite at a loss to explain the feeling of disappointment persisted. He carried it with him on a solitary walk along the cliffs the next Sunday morning. It was a day of blustering wind, and when he reached the headland that forms the northern point of Marsett Bay the sound of the surf far below was so loud that he was unaware of approaching footsteps until a voice said close to his ear, 'Good morning, sir!'

It was Inspector Mallett, his cheerful red face gleaming with the exertion of his walk, his moustache points limp in the salt-laden air. Pettigrew felt that he had never seen a healthier-looking man. 'Eupeptic,' he decided, was the only adjective that fitted him. The impression that he gave the inspector was not the same.

'If I may say so, Mr Pettigrew,' Mallett remarked, 'you're not looking quite the thing today. Not bad news, I hope?'

'Not at all, Inspector. Rather the reverse, if anything.'

'Indeed! I'm glad to hear that,' Mallett replied in disbelieving tones. 'Which reminds me, sir, I don't seem to have had any news from you about my little business.'

'I'm afraid not. I have been pretty busy over my own work lately.'

'So I gathered, sir. You and Miss Brown have had your work cut out, I understand.'

Pettigrew looked at him sharply, but the detective's face seemed entirely innocent of any double meaning that might be attached to his words.

'Yes,' he agreed, 'we have. But we seem to be through the worst of it now. And what about your inquiries?'

'I can't say that we're through the worst of them yet, sir. All the same, I think I may say we are progressing.' He looked up at the sky. 'It looks as though it might come on to rain,' he observed. 'Do you think we ought to be getting back?'

They left the headland and took the path back towards the town.

'Yes, we are progressing,' Mallett continued. 'We're some way from getting at the root of the trouble, but we have established that there are two departments in the Control involved – not the whole departments of course, I mean, but individuals in two different jobs who must be working together. And without turning the whole place upside down and upsetting everybody – which we don't want to do and Mr Palafox won't hear of anyway – it's very difficult to ascertain just who is involved. Meanwhile, I've been running about the country in the last week or two, and on the way I've unearthed what looks like a very pretty little Black Market affair which affects the Control. Your Enforcement Branch is working on it now, and I dare say it will come your way for an opinion before long.'

'That will be delightful,' said Pettigrew unenthusiastically.

Mallett caught the implication in his tone.

'Ah, sir!' he said. 'It's dull work, all these offences against Orders and Regulations. I'd sooner do a nice murder any day, wouldn't you, Mr Pettigrew? Give me regular crime every time!'

'The war has certainly produced a fine new crop of offences,' replied Pettigrew. 'And an astonishingly large number of people only too eager to commit them. I sometimes wonder whether there are any honest people left.'

'I wouldn't say that, sir,' said the inspector judicially, 'but I tell you what – there aren't enough honest people to go round.'

They talked of indifferent matters until they reached the outskirts of Marsett Bay. Then Pettigrew remembered a question he had been meaning to ask for some time.

'I was very much impressed the other evening,' he began, 'by the amount you and Jellaby seemed to know about all the people working at the Control.'

Mallett permitted himself to chuckle quietly.

'Not all of them, Mr Pettigrew,' he said. 'I'm afraid we were rather showing off that time. The fact is, we had been making rather a study of the Fernlea crowd.'

'Is that where you expect to find the people you are looking for?'

'That would be telling, sir. I don't want to embarrass you by putting suspicions in your mind about the people you are meeting every day and passing the salt to at breakfast. You'd find it very uncomfortable.'

Pettigrew needed no telling how very uncomfortable such a situation was.

'I quite understand,' he said. 'But that wasn't what I really meant to ask you. It occurred to me after I left you at the Gamecock that there was one of the Fernlea people whom you never mentioned.'

'Was there, sir?'

'Yes – Miss Danville.'

'Oh, bless my soul, Miss Danville! She's all right. At least – –' he grinned. 'She's an innocent so far as the trade is concerned. I sometimes wonder where the Government picks them up, I do really.'

And no more about Miss Danville could Pettigrew get from him.

They parted under the first scattered drops of rain in the High Street.

'Good day, sir,' said Mallett. 'I hope you've enjoyed your walk as much as I have. It gives one a wonderful appetite, that sea air. If only there were something waiting on the table to make an appetite worth while!'

Pettigrew, who knew the inspector's reputation as a trencherman, expressed his sympathy.

Mallett sighed. 'There's a little café in Bridge Street, the second turning on the left from here,' he said. 'It's just due for a prosecution under the Food Regulations,

Mr Jellaby tells me. I think it would be worth your while to visit it, sir, before it's too late. They say the stuff there is wonderful. As a policeman,' he concluded dolorously, 'I can't very well be seen inside it myself.'

## CHAPTER EIGHT

### Noises in the Corridor

As the inspector had said, the investigation into breaches of the Orders governing the Manufacture, Marketing, and Distribution of Pins was a dull business, even when dignified by the glamorous title of the Black Market. Pettigrew found it difficult to maintain any interest in the subject, in spite of the fact that he might now reasonably suspect that it concerned one or more of his immediate circle at the Control. On the other hand, the relationships between the same persons, as individuals, continued to provide problems which, while they often irritated him, he could not ignore. To his annoyance, they had begun to invade the office itself, instead of being confined to off-duty hours at Fernlea.

This new development manifested itself first in a number of small disturbances outside the door of his room. The mansion which housed the Control was not, generally speaking, a quiet place, but Pettigrew had the good fortune to be situated at the quietest end of it. Between him and the echoing halls where the main work of the departments was carried on lay the cloakrooms for the female staff and the little room that housed Miss Danville's strident kettle. Opposite these was a staircase leading up to the Registry. On his other side dwelt only the Controller and his immediate assistants. Partly because they were naturally dignified and sedate personages and partly because their rank demanded the provision of rugs and carpets even in the corridors leading to their offices, very little sound proceeded from this side. There was not much traffic past Pettigrew's door. Visitors to the Controller from outside used a side entrance farther down the corridor, and except for an occasional messenger few of the rank and file had occasion to penetrate to the august regions at the end of it. From his desk Pettigrew could hear, if he listened for it, the distant rumour of coming and going in the big rooms and the frequent footsteps of messengers ascending and descending the staircase. Otherwise, he was seldom disturbed.

It was not the noise itself that he objected to, for it was slight enough and only occurred at fairly long intervals, but rather to the fact that it did not seem to fit in with the regular sounds of the office, and he was in a mood to find anything irregular vaguely sinister. He knew the routine of the place by heart now, and could tell just when to expect the footsteps of the messenger bringing the morning's post into Miss Brown's room, or the firm, departmental tread of the Controller going to the canteen for his lunch. But these sounds were different. He could not relate them to any official activity at all. They seemed largely to consist of furtive advances and retreats, varied by murmured conversations which took place sometimes in the corridor itself, and sometimes (so far as he could judge) in the cubby-hole where tea was brewed.

Now that he was not so busy, Pettigrew had leisure to be distracted by these things, but it was some time before he aroused himself sufficiently to take any steps about them. Several times he was on the verge of questioning Miss Brown, but he had decided that for the time being it would be safer to confine their intercourse to purely official matters. Exactly in what way it was 'safer', he did not define to himself. At last, he determined to investigate on his own account, and this he did in the simplest method possible. One afternoon, when the mysterious noises were at their height, he walked abruptly out of his room and flung open the door leading into the corridor. Perhaps it was the long training of the London street crossings that made him automatically look first to his right, in the direction of the Controller's room. He was just in time to get a fleeting glimpse of the figure of a man bent double at the Controller's door, apparently in the act of looking through the keyhole.

His mind had barely time to register the sight before the man had straightened himself, and, hands in pockets, began strolling quietly towards him with an excellent assumption of ease. The light was behind him, and it was not until he was quite close that he could be recognized. It was Wood.

'Good afternoon,' said Wood when he reached Pettigrew, in a tone which might have been intended to be casual, but succeeded in sounding rather sheepish.

'Good afternoon,' Pettigrew echoed. There seemed to be nothing else to say.

Wood was about to walk on, when from behind the open door a high-pitched giggle suddenly made itself heard. It had a familiar ring, and Pettigrew was not surprised when Mrs Hopkinson emerged, holding a handkerchief to her mouth, her face red with ill-suppressed laughter.

'Are there any more of your friends about?' he asked Wood. He tried to make the question sound as disagreeable as possible. Marsett Bay, from being a bore, seemed fast becoming a Bedlam, and he did not feel at all like suffering these particular Bedlamites gladly.

Wood's assurance, he was glad to note, had begun to desert him.

'Would you – would you please not talk too loud?' he

murmured. 'You see, we're not supposed to be here, and – and – –'

Pettigrew had no intention of helping him out, and the Merry Widow seemed quite incapable of speech. He might have continued to splutter indefinitely if assistance had not come from elsewhere.

'I'm afraid we're in rather a spot,' said a suave voice, as Edelman emerged from the pantry next door. 'Would you mind very much, old fellow, if we all came into your room for a moment? This is a bit public.'

Pettigrew minded very much being called 'old fellow' by Edelman at that moment, but none the less he allowed himself to be swept back into his room with the three intruders close on his heels. Recovering the initiative, he quickly entrenched himself behind his desk and sat down. Once safely there, he felt himself in a judicial position from which he could regard the trespassers with a proper air of superiority.

'I think,' Edelman began in an easy manner, 'that the moment has arrived, in the classic phrase, to tell all.'

Pettigrew judged that the fatuity of this remark would be best underlined by making no reply to it. He accordingly remained silent, and waited for Edelman to try again.

'It is rather a ridiculous position to find oneself in,' the latter continued. 'The fact is, Wood was trying out a little experiment and Mrs Hopkinson and I were engaged meanwhile in – how shall I put it – –?'

'Keeping cave,' the Merry Widow interposed with a giggle.

'Er – yes, I think that that schoolboy expression does just about describe this rather schoolboyish episode. Wood was naturally anxious not to be detected in an action that was rather apt to be misconstrued, and – –'

Pettigrew began to lose patience.

'If you mean he didn't want to be seen looking through the Controller's keyhole, I can quite believe you,' he said. 'But would you oblige me now by cutting the cackle and telling me exactly what you were all up to?'

'Up to?' Mrs Hopkinson broke in. 'D'you mean you didn't tumble to it? We were rehearsing the giddy plot, of course!'

Pettigrew looked in bewilderment from one to another of the three faces confronting him.

'I think it's up to me to explain, as I'm really responsible,' Wood said. 'It's a little difficult for anyone who isn't himself a writer to appreciate the position, but I have always rather prided myself on getting my facts right. I – I belong to the realist school of fiction, I suppose, if you like to put it that way. Or perhaps you might say I'm even a bit deficient in imagination. The point is, I simply cannot write about a thing or place until I've seen it for myself. I must have a factual background to my stories, and to get that I sometimes stray into rather queer situations. Perhaps you'll understand the difficulty when I tell you that while I was getting material for *Death on the Bakerloo* I was twice arrested for trespassing on the Underground – –'

'Begging everyone's pardon for the interruption,' said Mrs Hopkinson, 'but if I don't run along now, I shall have Judith on my tail next minute! It's all very well for Mr Edelman, who's a law to himself, and everyone knows how slack Enforcement is, but it's rather different for poor little me. She thinks I'm in the you know what – –' she nodded in the direction of the ladies' cloakroom, 'but you can't spend half the day there, can you? Cheerybye, Mr Pettigrew! you won't be a spoilsport, will you?'

'Let me get this clear,' said Pettigrew after she had

gone. 'I don't see that it is any concern of mine, really, but as you have started to explain I think the explanation should be complete. So I understand, Wood, that you are investigating the possibilities of this part of the building as a setting for a crime story?'

'That's it, exactly,' Wood agreed. 'You'll remember, the first evening this idea was ever discussed, you suggested yourself what an admirable spot for the crime the library would be. Well, I've only been in the room once, and I simply had to have another squint at it.'

'Besides,' Edelman added, 'it was essential to the plot to know just how much of the room could be seen by an observer through the keyhole.'

'Exactly. Then we had to try all this out under actual conditions. I was very much worried with the problem of how to get my murderer to the library without being seen. This needed a good deal of study on the spot.'

'We had to find out just who was liable to go along that corridor at different times of the day, and when — study the routes of messengers and so on,' said Edelman. 'Find out when the Controller was most likely to be alone — —'

'Devise the getaway,' Wood put in. The pair were picking up each other's cues now like a couple of well-trained comedians.

'But,' Pettigrew expostulated, 'this is sheer, unadulterated nonsense! If you want to write a book surely you arrange the geography of your background and the movements of your characters to suit the plot, not vice versa. Do you really expect me to credit all this?'

'In a sense,' said Edelman after rather a long pause, 'that is a perfectly valid piece of criticism, I admit. But you see, we're not exactly writing a book at the moment.'

'I thought that was what you were telling me you were doing, Wood.'

'I can't answer for Wood, of course,' Edelman continued before Wood had time to say anything. 'He is a writer and I am not. So far as my part in it is concerned, we were simply doing what Mrs Hopkinson said just now – rehearsing the plot. We were seeing whether it would be possible to carry out in practice the fictitious crime which we have been engaged in devising. After all, it would be a waste of time to work out a thing of this kind *in vacuo* if you were not going to see whether it could be put into practice.'

'The whole thing is a waste of time, so far as I can see,' said Pettigrew. 'And – –'

But Edelman, with raised forefinger, motioned him to be silent. From the little room next door the kettle was whistling quietly, getting up steam for its full-voiced scream. Edelman looked at his watch and turned to Wood.

'Ten and a half minutes,' he said. 'I think that will just allow time for everything.' Then, as Miss Danville's hurried steps were heard, he went on, 'Here she comes, the deed completed. And during all this time, observe, nobody but ourselves has been down the corridor. It really works out very well.'

'Why on earth must you drag Miss Danville into your imbecilities?'

'Well, we agreed that she should be the murderer, didn't we? Besides, if you insist on being so matter-of-fact, she is quite capable of killing the Controller – or anyone else for that matter – if she's handled the right way. She's extremely suggestible. I know that from personal experience.'

Wood murmured something to Edelman which Pettigrew could not catch.

'Ah, yes! Wood reminds me that your secretary, who disapproves of our activities, will no doubt be bringing

in your tea directly, so we had better make ourselves
scarce, with apologies for having taken up your time. I
think I can promise that you are not likely to be disturbed again by any rehearsals. We have fixed everything now – even to the weapon. I ought just to tell you
about that, as you are so curious as to our doings. You
must have noticed those long skewer things the clerks
use for making holes in papers to tie the files up with.
Pointed and very sharp. Known locally as bodkins.
We've decided on one of those. It seems so entirely
appropriate, don't you think? And now, we must be off.
Once more, our apologies.'

Over his tea, which came with such suspicious
promptitude after the intruders' departure as to suggest
that Miss Brown was aware of their visit, Pettigrew reflected on the extraordinary story he had just heard.
The more he thought about it, the harder he found it
to believe. On consideration, he was most perplexed by
Edelman's part in the affair. He had made himself the
principal apologist, and seemed to have gone out of his
way to take the words out of the mouths of the others.
But could he really be devoting part of his working
hours to such an absurd, time-wasting scheme? Mrs
Hopkinson was different. Pettigrew judged her to be an
addle-pated creature, to whom one form of what she
called 'fun and games' was as good as another. Wood
was an author; and all writers were a little cracked in
one way or another. But if Edelman was anything, he
was a prodigious worker. It seemed utterly out of character for him to neglect his job in so purposeless a fashion.
And yet, if he was not telling the truth, what conceivable explanation for his behaviour could there be?

Pettigrew frowned. He had the uneasy impression
that Edelman was not a man who did things without
some object, and he was by no means convinced that

his objects would necessarily be desirable ones. He particularly disliked his easy reference to Miss Danville's suggestibility. It tied up with his calm appraisal of the chances of her being seriously affected should she get to learn of the part allotted to her in the plot. Was it possible that for some reason the fellow intended some harm to that poor vulnerable soul? And if so, to what end?

He shook himself. This positively would not do! Once more he was beginning to indulge in melodramatic suspicions about his fellows, and with even less cause than on the last occasion. It wasn't like him. Decidedly the atmosphere of Marsett Bay was beginning to affect him. To calm himself, he took up the file which had reached him just before he had surprised Wood at the Controller's door. He saw with interest that his opinion was required on the advisability of taking proceedings for a serious case of unlawful trading. Evidently this was the matter which Mallett had spoken of at their last meeting. The firm's name, he observed, was Blenkinsop. It seemed vaguely familiar. Then he recollected having heard the words 'the Blenkinsop file' being uttered in various tones of annoyance and reproof by Miss Clarke at the Fernlea, though in what connexion he could not say.

· Presently he was absorbed in Mallett's report, which was certainly a model of its kind. The case clearly had possibilities, but it was too intricate to master at a sitting at the fag-end of the day. Still he read on, hoping at least to have some general picture of the case to work on when he came to tackle it in detail on the morrow. But before long, he found himself distracted by noises outside his door. They were familiar noises too – the shuffling of feet, the murmur of voices, the ripple of suppressed laughter.... Really it was too much! He had

hardly expected Edelman and Wood to keep their promise that he should not be further disturbed, but to
break it within an hour was simply insulting.

In a mood of quiet fury, he once more strode to his
door and threw it open. But this time it was not to see
anybody at the door of the Controller's room. What he
saw instead was his own secretary's door hurriedly clos-
ing and Mr Phillips, rather pink in the face, walking
quickly away from it.

Pettigrew went back to his room as quickly as he
could. This was the last thing in the world he could have
wished to happen. To find himself caught spying on
Miss Brown's private affairs, even by the merest accident, was simply degrading. What on earth would she
think of him? He felt like rushing into her room to
apologize for his behaviour, but that would only make
matters worse. She would probably want to apologize
too and that would be unbearable. It was entirely
Phillips's fault, of course, but that didn't make things
any better. Damn Phillips! Damn Edelman! Damn the
Control and everything connected with it, including the
Blenkinsop file! A great wave of nostalgia for the
Temple swept over him. He felt utterly miserable.

CHAPTER NINE

## *The Balloon Goes Up*

ALTHOUGH Miss Brown confronted him next morning with unruffled calm, it was with some relief that Pettigrew heard her announce that she had been granted three days' leave and would be catching the afternoon train for London that day. He politely wished her an enjoyable holiday, and in answer to her apologies for the short notice assured her that in the present state of the legal adviser's work her absence would not cause him any undue inconvenience.

'I congratulate you on getting even such a small instalment of freedom,' he said. 'The Establishment Officer brutally told me that I am not entitled to any leave this side of Christmas.'

'Neither am I, really,' Miss Brown told him. 'I got him to give me this as a special concession.'

'Oh, yes?'

Pettigrew felt he had had quite enough of Miss Brown's private affairs, and was determined not to ask her by what plea she had managed to soften the heart of authority; but she continued, 'I didn't like to bother you, Mr Pettigrew, but I got particulars from those other insurance people you mentioned, and Tom and I agreed that the Empyrean terms suited me best.'

Tom? Oh, of course, that was Phillips's name. Funny he had never heard her call him that before.

'They want a medical examination, so I persuaded the Establishment Officer to advance me leave to go up for it.'

'I must say that was very clever of you. The Establishment Officer always sounds such a solid piece of work, but you seem to have found a soft spot in the structure somewhere. A bit of the cement that hadn't set properly, or something. Well, when do we meet again? Let me see, today's Tuesday. Your leave runs from Wednesday, I suppose. That carries you on to Saturday. I shall expect you on Monday, then, to tidy up the messes I shall make between now and then.'

Miss Brown shook her head.

'My leave runs from midday today,' she said. 'Strictly, I ought to be back in the office by noon on Friday. I've been allowed to stay away till Friday night, but I must be working again on Saturday morning.'

'Monstrous!' said Pettigrew. 'I take back what I said about the soft spot. The man must be ferro-concrete right through.'

'It doesn't matter much to me,' answered Miss Brown. 'Besides the examination, there's only a little shopping I want to get done, and I can fit it in quite easily. I shall be glad of the extra day's leave later on, I expect.'

It suddenly occurred to Pettigrew what the object of the little shopping was, and the purpose to which the extra day's leave would be devoted later on. For some reason, the idea of her going off alone to insure her life and buy her meagre wartime trousseau preparatory to spending the balance of her leave on a honeymoon with Phillips struck him as pathetic. But there was nothing he could do about it, except to disguise from her the fact that she was an object of sympathy.

'Well,' he said, 'at least there's no reason why you should waste any more time in the office this morning. No, don't tell me that it isn't midday yet. There's nothing to be done that can't very well wait till you get back.'

'I was going to index the Board of Trade memoranda

on Colonial Preference,' Miss Brown began doubtfully, but he cut her short.

'My dear girl, if the expression was not slightly blasphemous in this place, I should say that I don't care two pins for the Board of Trade memoranda. Be off with you. Get some sandwiches at the Black Market café in Bridge Street and be at the station in good time. Then you may get a seat, if the ruffians from the Contract Ministry haven't filled the train up at Greenlake.'

And having got rid of his secretary with a greater sense of relief than he would ever have thought possible, he settled down to a quiet morning's study of the delinquencies of the firm of Blenkinsop.

On the whole, the period of Miss Brown's absence passed better for Pettigrew than he had expected. Only once did he try the experiment of sending through to the pool for a shorthand writer. His call produced a smart young person with a pretty face. Pettigrew could not place her, but she vaguely reminded him of some unpleasant incident in the past that was only just over the borders of his memory. He remembered what it was the instant that she left the room; for outside his door he heard the vulgar, confident voice of Rickaby, complaining that he had been waiting there ten minutes to take her to lunch.

He felt that it only wanted Rickaby to make his corridor, which he had once thought so sequestered, the resort of all the imbeciles in the Control. Thereafter, he abjured any substitute for Miss Brown and contented himself with compiling sheets of scrawled manuscript for her to decipher on her return. The telephone gave him less trouble. To any caller who sounded tiresome he ejaculated gruffly, and truthfully, 'Mr Pettigrew's secretary is out. Is there any message?' Very few people, he was gratified to note, cared to entrust their messages to a mere secretary's deputy, and a surly one at that.

Life at the Fernlea, too, seemed to have become for the time being distinctly more civilized. On Tuesday night, Wood dined out with friends, with the result that the Plot, deprived of its arch-plotter, failed to establish itself against the rival attraction of the Brains Trust. Later, Edelman, who had (in his own words) been Joaded into it, treated the company to a brilliant and perverse onslaught on every kind of social and political reform. His display of verbal pyrotechnics was cut short by the belated entrance of Mrs Hopkinson, slightly drunk. Unlike any other woman Pettigrew had ever met, she was distinctly the better for being in liquor. Her unbridled cheerfulness communicated itself to the others, and before they quite knew how it had happened, they were all sitting down playing Racing Demon with ferocious abandon. The game went on till long past the usual decorous Fernlea hours and broke up at last with Phillips a pronounced winner. The next evening, Miss Clarke and the Merry Widow went to the cinema, while Rickaby took himself off to the White Hart. The four remaining men played an amicable rubber of bridge, with cards slightly creased by the orgy of the preceding night, leaving Miss Danville in peaceful contemplation of her devotional book. As he went up to bed afterwards, Pettigrew reflected that he had enjoyed the last two evenings more than any others since he had been at Marsett Bay. Chronic ill luck had made him something of a pessimist, and he found himself wondering whether this was not altogether too good to last.

It was. On Thursday it was evident at dinner that Miss Clarke had had a bad day at the office. She had come into violent collision with the Assistant Controller, and was now disposed to work off her bad temper on anyone within reach. The atmosphere in the lounge afterwards was sultry. Mrs Hopkinson appeared as usual, but on this occasion she was not only completely sober but also entirely lacking in her usual *bonhomie*. Pettigrew, who had some experience in such matters, judged her to be suffering from a delayed hangover. For once, she seemed disposed to carry over beyond office hours some dreary argument that had arisen during the day, and she and Miss Clarke bickered at length and with acrimony. Presently Phillips announced his intention of going upstairs to do some work and left the room. Scarcely was the door shut behind him before Mrs Hopkinson and Miss Clarke joined forces in abusing him. Their attack was upon lines that were to Pettigrew painfully familiar. Phillips was a sly designing brute, who had got that poor silly Brown girl into his clutches. It was a scandal that ought to be stopped, and a great pity that there was nobody to warn her of what she was doing. And so on.

Miss Danville, who was normally far too nervous of Miss Clarke to intervene in any discussion to which she was a party, here plucked up courage to defend Phillips. She thought he was an extremely nice, considerate, affectionate man, and Miss Brown was fortunate to have won the affection of anyone so worthy. At this, Miss Clarke merely sniffed and indicated that Miss Danville's opinion of Mr Phillips or anyone else carried no weight with her. Mrs Hopkinson, on the other hand, suddenly launched into a violent assault on the hapless Miss Danville. It was she, as everyone knew, who was responsible for the state of affairs, she who for some dark reasons of her own was trying to drive an ignorant girl into the arms of a man who was no better than a Mormon.

'How can you say such things?' Miss Danville protested, pale and shaken.

'A Mormon!' repeated Mrs Hopkinson. 'That's what he is! Calls himself a widower, indeed! That's what they all do! I know for a fact that he has a wife living – yes, and three kids too, poor deserted mites. He means to be the ruin of that girl, and you will be the one that's responsible!'

'It's not true! It's not true!' cried Miss Danville, by now almost in tears.

The altercation, which had begun in one corner of the room with angry *sotto voce* splutters and hisses, had by this time become loud enough to attract the attention of the other occupants of the lounge. Pettigrew, who had been trying to write a letter at the further end, heard Mrs Hopkinson's last assertion and felt that it was time to intervene.

'You really mustn't say things like that,' he said sternly, coming over to the warring ladies. 'If you start making accusations of that kind, Mrs Hopkinson, you may find yourself in very serious trouble.'

'It's perfectly true,' Mrs Hopkinson persisted.

'Indeed? Perhaps you'll tell me what evidence you have to support it?'

'Everybody knows it,' said Mrs Hopkinson sullenly. 'It's no good talking that lawyer's language about evidence.'

'I am going to talk some more lawyer's language to you,' Pettigrew replied sternly, 'and I hope for your sake you will understand it. You have just accused Mr Phillips of attempting to commit bigamy – a very grave criminal offence. If anyone chooses to repeat to him what you have said, you may be sued for slander and ordered to pay damages which would ruin you for life. Do I make myself clear?'

The effect on Mrs Hopkinson was gratifying. She turned extremely red, muttered something which Pettigrew could not catch and finally joined Miss Clarke, who had retreated to the other side of the room. It was an easy triumph, but Pettigrew could not but feel a qualm as he reflected that she had after all done little more than put into words with a few picturesque trimmings the very thoughts which he had himself been entertaining only a short time before.

'It isn't true, Mr Pettigrew! Tell me it isn't true!'

Miss Danville's plaintive voice recalled him to his surroundings. She was thoroughly upset, her large, dark eyes brimming with tears and her hands fumbling uncertainly in her bag for a handkerchief.

'No,' said Pettigrew kindly, sitting down beside her on the sofa. 'It isn't true. Why should it be? Don't think of it again.'

But she was not so readily to be comforted.

'It's easy to say that,' she wailed, 'but you don't *know*. There's no smoke without fire, and if it wasn't true, why should Mrs Hopkinson – –'

'I have no idea why Mrs Hopkinson should have behaved as she did, except that she was in a mood for making mischief. As for there being no smoke without fire, I think it is the silliest proverb ever invented. It is the tale-bearer's charter. Every credulous gossip-monger trots it out as an excuse – –'

He realized that he was wasting his breath. Miss Danville was beyond the reach of argument. An idea had been lodged in her crazy brain and mere reason could not remove it. Basely Pettigrew tried another way.

'It is very un-Christian to harbour such suspicions about another,' he said.

Miss Danville's face lighted up.

'Yes!' she murmured. 'I shall pray – I shall pray. . . . But oh!' she went on, turning towards him, 'if I could only have some positive assurance that I had not done a dreadful wrong to that poor girl! If someone could only tell me that they know it isn't true?'

'I can tell you,' Pettigrew said solemnly. 'I know that it isn't true.'

'You *know*?'

'I know for a fact that Mr Phillips is a widower. You can set your mind at rest about that.'

'Thank you, thank you, Mr Pettigrew!' Then her face clouded again with doubt. 'You're not just saying this to comfort me?' she asked piteously. 'You have – what was the expression you used just now? – you have evidence of it?'

'Yes, I have evidence.'

She sighed with relief. Then she laid her hand on his arm and murmured. 'Please forgive me, but I have been so upset. If it isn't too much to ask, may I see your evidence? Then I shan't need ever to worry about this again.'

Pettigrew hesitated for a moment, but his sympathy with Miss Danville was too strong to be denied. At all costs, he felt, he must kill this dangerous slander. Besides, to be called as a witness in an action for defamation was the very last thing he desired. It was worth risking a breach of confidence to avoid it. His private papers were in a little attaché case which he had left by the writing-table. He fetched it, took from it the copy of Tillotson's letter and handed it to her.

'Here is your evidence,' he said. It was fortunate, he felt, that Miss Danville would not be likely to inquire how it came into his hands, and still less likely to make nice distinctions between the evidential value of a copy letter and an original.

Miss Danville read the letter slowly, her lips forming the words as she did so. In her overwrought state, Pettigrew was prepared for her to show some emotion at finding the grotesque charge against Phillips disproved in black and white; but the effect was more violent than he had expected. At the first sentence of the letter she broke into a radiant smile, but by the time she had reached the end of the paragraph she was in floods of tears.

Pettigrew, not for the first time since he had come to Marsett Bay, felt horribly embarrassed. He could find no words to comfort her. After all, he had already provided the comfort, and if the result was this outpouring, there was nothing he could do except to wait and hope that she would soon stop crying and behave sensibly. If only Miss Brown had been there! She could handle Miss Danville as nobody else could, or cared to do. But then, if she had been there, it was tolerably certain that this wretched situation would never have arisen at all.

Miss Danville solved the problem, not by stopping crying, but by leaving the room, mopping her eyes with a sodden handkerchief as she went. Pettigrew hastily recovered his 'evidence' to put it away. At that moment Mrs Hopkinson, who must have been watching him from across the room, came over to him. Pettigrew looked at her sourly, but she seemed determined to make an effort at appeasement.

'Sorry about all this shemozzle,' she said. 'Just when we'd been getting a bit matey, too. My fault, but I do get het up about things sometimes. I've got a wicked tongue, I know, but I'm like that.'

Pettigrew felt too disgusted with her to say anything. He put the letter away in his attaché case and closed the lock with a vicious snap. But Mrs Hopkinson was not to be denied.

'You're such a sport, Mr Pettigrew,' she pleaded. 'You won't tell on me to Mr Phillips, will you? I should just hate to be prosecuted for thousands of pounds damages – even if I had them. What a hope!' she added with a giggle.

'I propose to forget all about this incident as soon as

I can, and I advise you to do the same,' said Pettigrew stiffly.

'There! I *knew* you'd be a sport. Well, that's a load off my little chest, anyway – but, ooh! I was forgetting! What about Miss Danville? D'you think she'll split on me?'

'Naturally, I can't answer for Miss Danville.'

'That old looney would say anything,' said Mrs Hopkinson peevishly. 'Look at the state she was in just now – laughing and crying all at once.'

'You have yourself to thank for that, Mrs Hopkinson.'

Mrs Hopkinson chose to be indignant in her turn.

'I like that!' she exclaimed. 'Why, it was you that set her off. I saw you. Showing her letters and things!'

Pettigrew had striven to keep cool, but this was too much for his self-control.

'This conversation has gone on quite long enough,' he said. 'I am not going to stand here to be accused by you. After you had thoroughly upset Miss Danville with your wild talk, I had to do my best to undo the mischief. As for the letter I gave her to read, it may interest you to know that it was from the late Mrs Phillips's solicitor, confirming the fact of her death.'

He was sorry to have had to say so much, but he felt it was worth it to see Mrs Hopkinson's face.

'Crikey!' she exclaimed. 'I *am* in a mess, aren't I? She's bound to tell him, or that Brown girl, which is all the same thing. What d'you think I'd best do, Mr Pettigrew?'

'I really cannot advise you. If you've got yourself into trouble by your intemperate language, you must get out of it as best you can.'

'That's right!' Mrs Hopkinson snapped back. 'Kick a girl when she's down! Isn't that a man all over? Anyhow,' she went on, 'I know what I shall do without any of your advising, thank you! The very next chance I get,

I'm going to tell Mr Phillips the whole story and ask his pardon before either of those women can get at him. He won't have the face to do anything to me after that.'

Pettigrew felt extremely doubtful of the wisdom of such a course, but in face of what he had just said, he could hardly express an opinion. He therefore watched in silence while Mrs Hopkinson retired to the other end of the room and, after some hesitation, joined the little circle round the fire.

Here meanwhile, apparently too engrossed in their own concerns to have taken more than a passing interest in what was going on elsewhere, Edelman and Miss Clarke were listening with close attention to Wood, who was evidently winding up an exposition of the Plot.

'So I think the whole thing is fairly cut and dried,' he was saying.

It was curious, Pettigrew noticed, how confident and authoritative he was, now that he was dealing with his own subject, in contrast to the modesty which he had displayed when the question of his literary activities was first broached.

'Here's a plan of the scene of the crime,' he was saying. 'Only rough, I'm afraid, but it gives one an idea. And here's a time-table of the movements of all the suspects. There's an alibi for everyone, of course – or looks as if there was, at first sight. The only one I haven't quite worked out is Rickaby, but I'm proposing – –'

'Must we have Mr Rickaby in?' asked Miss Clarke. 'He does seem to me such an undesirable person in every way.'

'But we agreed to that, Miss Clarke, don't you remember. Besides, we really need him. Now what I suggest for Rickaby is – –'

'Who's taking my name in vain?' asked Rickaby, coming in at that moment. He had been drinking, and unlike Mrs Hopkinson, was not improved by the process. 'Who's – Oh, the Plot, I see! Now look here, fellows, I've just had a simply smashing idea. Came to me in the White Hart, and I simply careered all the way back to tell you. Listen. It really will simply knock you endways, I promise you. Honestly it will. Listen, I say. Why shouldn't old Pettigrew do this murder of ours? Pettigrew. He's the man. We've been leaving you out all this time, Pettigrew, and I say it's a shame. He's the man. Deep and sly and – and deep and everything. He's just – –'

'Don't be ridiculous, Rickaby,' said Edelman curtly. 'All this was settled weeks ago. The murder is to be committed by Miss Danville.'

'Oh! Miss Danville!' said Rickaby, as if he were hearing the name for the first time. 'Well, if you say so – Miss Danville. Mind you, I still think my notion's a dam' good one, don't you, Pettigrew? However, if you say so, I suppose it is so.'

'I think you had better go to bed, Mr Rickaby,' said Miss Clarke in the trumpet tone usually reserved for the office.

'Perhaps I had,' said Rickaby meekly. When Miss Clarke spoke to anyone in her office voice, the person spoken to had to be a good deal more drunk or of more determined character than Rickaby not to obey. Nevertheless, he contrived to assume a certain swagger as he walked to the door. He flung it open, to find himself confronted by Miss Danville, who was just coming in.

'Ah, here she is!' he exclaimed with tipsy politeness. 'We were just talking about you, Miss Danville!'

She paid no attention to him, but went across to where Pettigrew was standing. She was still pale, but her eyes were dry.

'Mr Pettigrew, I'm afraid you'll think I behaved very

stupidly just now,' she began in a low, hurried voice. 'After you had been so very kind to me. But I must – –'

Rickaby, still standing with the door-knob in his hand, felt that he was being ignored; and he was not in a mood to be ignored.

'It's no use your talking to old Pettigrew,' he interrupted. 'He's been turned down. I suggested him, but he's been turned down. You're the one who's been chosen.'

'Chosen?' asked Miss Danville. 'I don't understand. Chosen for what?'

'To do the murder, of course!'

'Be quiet, you young fool!' said Pettigrew. But it was too late.

'Don't you listen to him, Miss Danville,' Rickaby went on. 'He's only jealous because they wouldn't have him. You're to murder the Controller. It's all settled. Wood's arranged it. It's written down in the Plot. You ought to be jolly grateful to old Wood.'

But it was evident that Miss Danville was anything but grateful. A deep flush began to spread over her cheeks and she was trembling.

'So you want me to kill a man?' she said slowly, in a loud, deep voice, totally unlike her own.

Pettigrew tried once more to save the situation.

'This is nothing but a joke,' he said. 'A silly sort of story which these people have concocted – –'

'A joke?' Miss Danville repeated, her voice rising several tones. 'Do you men and women think death and the fear of death nothing but a joke? You' – she turned to Wood – 'who make murder your pastime, and spend your days devising ever fresh means to take the lives of your fellow creatures – and you' – she looked at Edelman, who was sitting back in his chair regarding her with an air of dispassionate interest – 'who tempted me and tried to send me to kill another woman, what have I done to you that you should persecute me? Oh, my God!' she screamed, 'is it for this that I have prayed to Thee to deliver me from the valley of the shadow of death – –'

'Miss Danville!' Only Miss Clarke's voice could have possibly made itself heard at that moment. 'Cease this nonsense at once! Are you mad?'

There was a moment's absolute silence, and then a horrible thing happened. Miss Danville began to laugh. Hideously and uncontrollably she laughed, with the tears running down her cheeks, a wavering finger pointing in Miss Clarke's direction.

'Perhaps I am,' she said at last. 'Perhaps I am. After all, I only left Chalkwood Asylum seven years ago!'

She turned to go. Phillips, evidently attracted by the noise from below, had entered a moment or two before. Bewildered by what he saw and heard, he went towards her to assist her; but she pushed him away almost violently and ran from the room.

# CHAPTER TEN

## *The Whistling Kettle*

BREAKFAST next morning at the Fernlea Residential Club was a more silent affair than usual, though, indeed, it was not ordinarily a talkative function. The scene of the night before had left a sense of guilt upon most of the participants. They munched and gulped stolidly, read their newspapers, and avoided one another's eyes. Miss Danville did not appear. Pettigrew ventured to ask Miss Clarke how she was, and was told that she had had a cup of tea sent up to her room, and thereafter locked the door.

'I spoke to her through the door,' Miss Clarke said. 'She said she didn't want anything. I invited her to apply for sick leave in the proper way, but she told me she felt much better and hoped to be at the office this morning. I'm sure I hope she will not. The position would be most awkward. I think that it is really my duty to speak to the Establishment Officer about her. If necessary, he must take the matter up with the Controller.'

Pettigrew murmured sympathetically. He appreciated Miss Clarke's difficulties, but his real sympathy was for Miss Danville. Obviously, her days with the Control were numbered. He felt that he would miss the poor harassed creature, and wondered what future there was for her in a world that had already used her so hardly.

During the morning, he was too busy to have much thought for the troubles of Miss Danville or anybody else. For the last two days he had been occupied in putting the finishing touches to the case against the peccant firm of Blenkinsop, and he now devoted himself to straightening out the last convulsions of that intricate affair before sending it to the prosecuting authorities in London. It would be the first prosecution since his appointment, and he was determined to do the Control credit. He broke off for lunch with the job half done, and went into the canteen, with figures, dates, and schedules still running in his head, punctuated by an orderly march of Statutory Rules and Orders, Directions, and all the stately paraphernalia of Control.

He was recalled to actuality when, midway through his meal, another tray was set down beside his own and he looked up to see Miss Danville taking her seat next to him. She appeared to be quite calm and normal, except that her thin lips were set in a straight line, giving her an unusual, and to Pettigrew rather alarming, air of determination. There was something about her that made him quite certain that she intended to unbosom herself to him, and the prospect filled him with dismay. More and more, and always against his will, he had found himself drawn into the private affairs of his colleagues at Marsett Bay. He was determined to go no further, if he could possibly avoid it. For the sake of his own peace of mind, he must choke Miss Danville off – gently if he could, brutally if he must. He quickly made up his mind to forestall her before she could begin.

'I am surprised to see you here today,' he said. 'I understood that you would not be coming to work. Do you think you were altogether wise?'

'Thank you, I am feeling better. Miss Clarke advised me to apply for sick leave, but I particularly wanted to come. I wanted the opportunity of seeing you, Mr Pettigrew, before this evening.'

Pettigrew deliberately ignored her last sentence.

'Honestly, I think you were unwise,' he said. 'You are

not looking at all strong. Don't you think a day in bed would be the best thing for you?'

Miss Danville shook her head.

'That was what Miss Clarke said,' she observed, as though that in itself was a sufficient answer to the suggestion.

'And I am sure she was right. I know that she is sometimes a little difficult to get on with, but in this matter I feel she was only thinking of what was good for you.'

'She has been very patient with me this morning,' Miss Danville admitted. 'She has only given me the simplest things to do, and asked me to go home early this afternoon. But I told her I must stay to make the tea for everyone as usual. It's about the only thing I do that seems to be of any use.'

'I should have thought that someone else could be found to do it for once,' Pettigrew observed, but Miss Danville was not to be sidetracked any longer.

'About last night,' she said abruptly. 'There's something important I must explain.'

'Please!' protested Pettigrew. 'I assure you there is nothing to explain – nothing at all.'

'But there *is*,' she persisted. 'I know you must have thought – –'

'I thought you were disgracefully treated, and you had my sympathy. That is all there is to it. I really don't think we can usefully discuss it any more.'

'I don't exactly want to *discuss* anything, Mr Pettigrew. I feel that I ought to tell you something about myself.'

'Listen,' said Pettigrew firmly. 'I don't know quite how clear your recollection of last night is, but during the course of the evening you – you let fall that at one time you had suffered from what is, after all, medically speaking, simply an illness of a particular type. I accept that as a fact, just as I would accept any other fact about an acquaintance.' His heart smote him as he saw Miss Danville shrink at the word. 'Or, shall I say, a friend of no very long standing?' he added hastily. 'But, to be quite frank, it is not a matter which I feel concerns me particularly, or on which I am in the least competent to give advice. So far as it affects your position here, it is a question between you and your official superiors. I don't want to seem lacking in sympathy, but I can do absolutely nothing about it. And now, if you'll excuse me, I must be getting back to my work.'

Feeling rather as though he had been hitting a child, he rose from the table.

'Please,' said Miss Danville, looking up at him almost despairingly. 'Will you tell me one thing? When is Miss Brown expected back?'

'This evening, so far as I know. Didn't she tell you?'

'Yes, I remember now, she did. But I forget things sometimes – like I did last night, until something reminds me – –'

'Look here,' said Pettigrew, relenting a little. 'If you want to talk your situation over with anyone, why don't you wait till she returns? After all, you are great friends, and you'll find it much more easy to speak to another woman about it than you would to me.'

'Yes, yes, I will. Of course I will,' Pettigrew heard her murmuring as he beat a hasty retreat.

It was with difficulty that Pettigrew wrenched his mind back from the problems of Danville to those of Blenkinsop when he got back to his room. Before he could do so, he went through an uneasy period during which he saw himself in the part of the Levite who passed by on the other side. But he was consoled by the thought that at least he knew, as the Levite did not, that the Good Samaritan was due on the evening train.

To those competent hands he was content to entrust the wayfarer. His conscience thus quietened, he worked steadily on through the afternoon, and the Blenkinsop papers were complete and in his 'Out' tray when the first tremulous pipe from the kettle next door told him that it was four o'clock.

During Miss Brown's absence on leave, Pettigrew had perforce gone without his tea. Perfect in all else, she had forgotten to make alternative arrangements for him. He could not make it for himself, as he had not succeeded in discovering where his tray and teapot were hidden. Consequently, the sound was on this occasion of interest to him only as marking the passage of time and not as heralding a break from labour. He paid little attention to it, but it struck him that the sound of Miss Danville's footsteps came more promptly than usual after the first notes; generally it was not until it was in full cry that she appeared. Then a curious thing happened. Instead of Miss Danville's arrival being followed by abrupt silence as the kettle went off the boil, the noise continued. It reached its loudest pitch. It continued at that pitch. It went on and on as though it would never stop. The whole building seemed to ring with the furious, insistent sound.

Just when he was beginning to wonder if he could stand the racket much longer, Pettigrew was surprised to see his door open and Miss Brown appear. She was without a hat, in her office clothes, and looked as though she had never been away.

'What is the meaning of this?' he asked her. 'You're not supposed to be at work till tomorrow. What will the Establishment Officer say?'

'It's the fault of the railway, really,' she replied. 'They have taken off the afternoon train from London, and I couldn't bear to take the last one and get here about midnight. So I caught the early train, and I thought I would fill in the time filing ––'

'The Board of Trade memoranda – I know. How single-minded your sex is.' Pettigrew could not resist adding, 'This will be rather a surprise for Mr Phillips.'

Miss Brown neither bridled nor blushed. 'I don't expect so,' she said calmly. 'I sent him a telegram to say I was coming early.'

'Well, it is a pleasant surprise for me, at any rate. Your first task is going to be to get me some tea. I have three days' sugar ration accumulated. But when is Miss Danville coming to stop this infernal row? I thought I heard her some time ago, but it must have been you. You were responsible for this horrible contraption. Please do something about it before my head splits.'

'I'll go and see.'

Miss Brown left the room. She was back again almost immediately.

'Will you come at once, please,' she said breathlessly. 'I think there's something wrong.'

Pettigrew followed her quickly into the corridor. Outside the pantry door they met Mrs Hopkinson coming from the direction of the Licensing Section.

'When are we going to get our giddy tea?' she shouted above the noise of the whistle. 'Is the Danville saying her prayers again or what?'

'I don't know what's happened,' said Miss Brown. 'I can't open the door.'

'Just what I said! She's gone off in a holy swoon, like she did once before, only this time she's locked herself in. Here, wake up!' and she hammered on the door.

Pettigrew turned the handle and put his shoulder to the door. It was certainly locked. Like most of Lord Eglwyswrw's furniture, it was strongly constructed, and he experienced a moment of helplessness as he pushed vainly against its solid resistance. He was relieved to see a messenger approaching down the corridor.

Messengers in Government departments do not usually hurry, and this one did not. He came up to the anxious little group at his ordinary steady pace, and stopped when he was abreast of them.

'Door locked?' he inquired.

'Yes,' said Pettigrew, exasperated. 'Help me break this down, will you? It may be urgent.'

The messenger deliberately put his load of papers on the floor and felt in his pocket. After some fumbling he produced a key.

'This opens most of them,' he announced, and fitted it in the lock.

The key turned and the door swung open. Pettigrew dashed in, followed by the two women. The little room was filled with steam escaping from the kettle, the lid of which was bouncing madly, while the whistle screamed like a locomotive entering a tunnel.

Miss Danville was kneeling, or rather crouching, on the floor, her head against the leg of the table on which the gas ring stood. 'What did I tell you?' shouted Mrs Hopkinson. 'She's at it again! Good Lord!'

As she spoke Miss Danville quietly collapsed sideways. Pettigrew was in time to catch her before she fell. Her face, he saw, was a dead white, and her breath came in deep, convulsive gasps.

'Mrs Hopkinson, there's a first aid post somewhere in the building, isn't there?' he cried. 'Go and get it. Miss Brown, telephone for an ambulance at once.'

Still supporting Miss Danville with one arm, he reached over with the other and turned off the gas. It suddenly became absolutely quiet in the tiny room.

Pettigrew became aware of the messenger at his elbow,

In the excitement of the moment he had forgotten him altogether.

'Better lay her down, sir, don't you think?' he suggested. 'And open the window to give her a bit of air.'

Pettigrew laid the sagging body down on the floor, and, kneeling down, supported her head in his arms. The messenger meanwhile flung the window open. It was obvious that Miss Danville was in a state of complete collapse, but he could see no apparent sign of any injury.

'I hope those first aid people won't be long,' he murmured.

'I know *them*,' observed the messenger contemptuously. 'Never at hand when they're wanted, and precious little use when they are there.' He came closer, looked at the figure on the floor and added. 'But I'm afraid there's not much that anyone could do in this case, if I'm not mistaken.'

As he spoke, Miss Danville's eyelids fluttered. She looked up at Pettigrew and something in her face told him that she recognized him. She murmured something and he bent his head to catch it. But the faint voice trailed away, and he could distinguish nothing. There was a slight tremor in her body and then her head fell back, a dead weight on his arm. For the second time that day Miss Danville had been unable to tell him what she wanted to say, and there was to be no third chance.

Whether because, as the messenger had said, the personnel of the first aid post were out of the way when their services were required, or because Miss Brown was more efficient in an emergency than Mrs Hopkinson, the ambulance arrived first on the scene. The frightened young woman in charge of the first aid post was several minutes behind and her appearance coincided with that of the doctor whom Miss Brown had also summoned on her own responsibility. By then, Miss Danville was already on a stretcher and the ambulance men were contemplating her with an air of resignation.

'I'm afraid she's gone, doctor,' said the leading ambulance man. 'We've been trying artificial respiration, but she doesn't respond.'

The doctor was very recently qualified, and he was honest enough to admit to himself that the man had a great deal more experience of death in its various manifestations than he. Nevertheless, he made a perfunctory examination. At the end of it, he nodded.

'What do you think was the cause of death, doctor?' asked Pettigrew. 'She was perfectly well a few hours ago.'

'I can't possibly tell you without a proper examination. There will have to be a post-mortem, of course.'

'And when will you do that?'

'I shan't. This matter will have to be reported to the coroner, and he is the person to order a post-mortem. It is the job of the county pathologist to carry it out. Now will you give me a few particulars about the deceased, please?'

A few minutes later the ambulance left, carrying Miss Danville's body to the mortuary. Pettigrew, as he saw it go, felt the feeling of self-reproach which had come over him after lunch return with double force. She had been so anxious to explain things to him, to confide in him, so pitifully hurt by his refusal. He felt no particular curiosity to know what it was that she had tried to say, but it hurt him very much to think that by listening to her he might have made the last few hours of her life a little happier. It was quite irrational, of course. How was he to know that the traveller would die before the Good Samaritan arrived? All the same – –

'Mr Pettigrew,' said Mrs Hopkinson just behind him, 'Mr Pettigrew, do you think it would be very awful of me if I went in there to make some tea? We do really want it badly, and after a shock like this – –'

'Of course,' Pettigrew said. 'I quite understand. Only, if you don't mind, I'd rather you took the whistle out of that kettle before you boil it up again.'

# CHAPTER ELEVEN

## The Missing Report

ON the whole, the sudden death of an unpopular member of a small circle is calculated to produce more depression than that of the greatest favourite. This was Pettigrew's reflection as he surveyed the lounge at the Fernlea that Friday evening. Miss Danville had been a butt, a nuisance, an object of ridicule. Now she had taken an unfair advantage of them all by suddenly becoming a tragic figure. Her former tormentors felt, inevitably, a sense of guilt and at the same time obscurely resentful towards her for putting them in the wrong. It was not easy to find words which would express a proper respect for the dead without at the same time sounding hopelessly false. The presence of Miss Brown, genuinely and speechlessly grief-stricken, made the position still more awkward for them. The result was one of the most silent evenings that Pettigrew could remember having endured since he had come to Marsett Bay.

The appearance of Mrs Hopkinson brought a little animation to the scene. She had fewer inhibitions than most people, and she had at least something concrete to talk about. She described at length for the benefit of everyone within the range of her voice exactly what she had seen and heard that afternoon, and at still greater length exactly how she had felt and what she had said about it.

'It was all so sudden, I just couldn't believe it had happened,' she said for the fifth time. 'She just collapsed and went over like *that*. And then I saw her face and it looked too ghastly! I'm sure I shan't sleep tonight.'

'Try not to think about it,' said Pettigrew, knowing quite well that this was the last thing she would want to do. She was, in fact, enjoying herself more than a little, whether she was aware of it or not.

'Do you suppose they'll make me give evidence at the inquest?' she asked hopefully.

'I should hardly think so. I don't really think you need worry yourself about that.'

Mrs Hopkinson sighed deeply, whether in disappointment or not it was hard to determine, and Pettigrew hoped that he had silenced her, but a moment later she began again.

'It was so *sudden*!' she repeated. 'What happened, do you think, Mr Pettigrew? Did her heart stop beating all at once?'

'I've no doubt it did,' said Pettigrew shortly. It was a fairly safe guess to make about anybody who was dead, he felt.

'I mean, what exactly did she die of?'

'Really, I haven't the least idea. We shall have to wait for the inquest to tell us that, obviously.'

'When do you suppose that will be?'

'Very soon, I have no doubt. I'm not very familiar with the way they arrange these things, but I suppose there will be a post-mortem examination at once, and after that the inquest. Until then, I don't really think there is anything to be gained by discussing this unhappy business.'

Pettigrew was a little out in his timing of the procedure. It so happened that on this particular Friday the coroner for the district was conducting an inquest some miles away. His car broke down on his way home, and in consequence the death of Miss Danville was not reported to him until late that night. Nothing in the report indicated any exceptional urgency about the case, and next day in the ordinary course he authorized the county pathologist to carry out a post-mortem examination to ascertain the cause of death. That hardworked official was instructed on Saturday morning, as he was on the point of leaving for a much needed weekend holiday. He therefore arranged with the coroner to perform his task on Monday morning, and the inquest was fixed for that afternoon.

At half-past ten on Monday morning, Police Constable James Gunn, the coroner's officer, entered the mortuary at Marsett Bay hospital to prepare the body of Honoria Danville for the examination.

At half-past ten on Monday morning, Pettigrew was surprised, but by no means displeased, by Miss Brown announcing that Inspector Mallett wished to see him. It was the first visit he had paid to his room, and Pettigrew made him welcome. The sight of that substantial figure on the opposite side of his desk seemed to bring a whiff of reality to the bloodless operations of the Pin Control.

'Your secretary doesn't look too good this morning, sir,' Mallett observed as he settled down gingerly on the narrow office chair.

'No. I'm afraid she's had rather a shock. We all have, indeed. But Miss Danville was a particular friend of hers.'

'Ah, yes, Miss Danville, I heard about that. A sad affair. But now, sir, about this business of ours — —'

'You mean, I suppose, the Blenkinsop prosecution, Inspector?'

Mallett looked surprised.

'Yes, of course,' he said. 'But — weren't you expecting me here this morning, Mr Pettigrew?'

'No, in point of fact I wasn't. Not that I'm not very glad to see you, of course.'

Pettigrew thought he could see something disapproving in the inspector's eye, and wondered in what way he could have offended.

'I see,' Mallett was saying. 'Of course, I can understand with all the upset about poor Miss Danville you won't have had time to read my report.'

'Certainly I've read your report,' Pettigrew protested. 'Some days ago, in fact. I've sent it to London, with the rest of the papers, recommending a prosecution.'

'My second report, I meant, sir.'

'I haven't seen any such thing.'

'That's very odd, sir,' said Mallett, pulling at his moustache. 'You should have had it on Friday.'

Pettigrew rang for Miss Brown.

'There are some papers missing in the Blenkinsop matter,' he told her. 'They came in on Friday, or should have done. Have you seen them anywhere?'

Miss Brown shook her head.

'There were no fresh papers in Blenkinsop on Friday,' she said positively. 'If there had been, I should have entered them in my register and put them with the others.'

'You are quite sure? You remember Friday was the day you came back from leave, and shortly after that, we – we were all rather concerned about other matters. Don't you think you may have overlooked them, or put them with the wrong file by mistake?'

'I am quite certain I didn't, Mr Pettigrew. You see, after Miss Danville – after Miss Danville was taken away, I was feeling rather upset, so to calm myself down I made a special effort to clear things up before I left the office. There were quite a number of papers that had come in while I was away, which hadn't been properly registered' – she looked at Pettigrew reproachfully – 'and I went through all those. Then I checked up all your files and saw that they were in order. I must have noticed if there were any loose Blenkinsop papers.'

'It's very strange,' said Mallett. 'I left my report with the Controller's secretary on Friday morning, and it was to be sent through to you direct. I nearly left it in this room myself, but she talked some mumbo-jumbo about sending a transit slip through to the Registry, and I thought I'd better conform to the office routine, more's the pity.'

'I suppose the Controller's secretary forgot about it, and it's there still,' said Pettigrew. 'Miss Brown, I think you'd better go along and make inquiries.'

Miss Brown was hardly out of the room before the telephone rang. Pettigrew answered it.

'It's for you,' he said, passing the instrument over to Mallett.

'Yes?' said Mallett into the telephone. 'Speaking. . . . She – what? . . . This is rather unexpected, Mr Jellaby. . . . Yes, I know, but it isn't my case, you appreciate that. I'm only here to. . . . Very well, but of course that's a matter for your Chief to decide with the Commissioner. . . . While I'm here, I'll keep an eye on things un-officially, but I can't possibly conduct the inquiry un-less. . . . Yes, certainly I'll tell him. . . . Yes, of course. . . . Certainly. I'll see you this afternoon, then. Good-bye.'

The inspector replaced the receiver, his face as im-passive as usual. But having done so, he pulled his moustache extremely hard, which was the only way in which he was ever known to express emotion.

'That was Inspector Jellaby,' he said. 'He was speak-ing about Miss Danville.'

'Yes?'

'Yes. There has been a rather surprising development in that case, Mr Pettigrew. You were one of the first people on the spot. Was there anything you noticed that suggested violence?'

'Violence? Certainly not. I thought she had had a seizure or something of the kind.'

'Well, when the coroner's officer stripped the body this morning for the pathologist to do his post-mortem, he found what appeared to be a stab wound in the centre of the abdomen.'

'Good heavens, Inspector, but surely this isn't possible! I was actually with the poor woman when she died, and I swear I noticed nothing.'

'Neither did the doctor who came at the time, apparently. Internal haemorrhage, I suppose, and no trace outside, except a small hole in her dress which nobody would see without looking for it. I have known such cases. We shan't know for certain till the pathologist makes his report, of course. But Mr Jellaby tells me you have been warned to attend the inquest this afternoon and he asked me to let you know what to expect.'

'But – this must be murder!'

'It certainly looks like it, sir. No doubt Mr Jellaby will want a full statement from you in due course. Your evidence may be important. But so far as the inquest goes, I should think that the coroner will now simply take evidence of identification and the medical evidence and then adjourn. So I dare say your evidence won't be wanted, at this court.'

Miss Brown came into the room at this point.

'The Controller's secretary is quite certain that the papers were marked out to you on Friday afternoon,' she said. Her face was rather pink, and Pettigrew, who had met the leathery, vinegary spinster who acted as the Controller's watchdog, knew without being told that there had been something of a scene when she was accused of mislaying documents.

'Thank you, Miss Brown,' he said and let her go. He

did not feel equal to discussing Mallett's ghastly news before her.

'This is rather a serious matter, Mr Pettigrew,' the inspector observed, as soon as Miss Brown had left.

'Serious? You are putting it very mildly, Inspector. Who on earth could have wanted to harm that poor, innocent creature?'

'I wasn't thinking of that, sir. I was talking about the report of mine that's missing.' Then, seeing Pettigrew's surprised expression, he went on, 'You see, sir, this affair of Miss Danville isn't my case. It may possibly become mine later on, and I've promised Mr Jellaby to give him a hand, unofficially, if I can. Whoever handles the case is going to regret these three days wasted with no inquiries made, and I don't envy him his job. But it isn't my affair. My affair, sir, is the Blenkinsop matter, and I say that the loss of my report is serious.'

Mallett emphasized his words by another tug at his moustache points.

Really, thought Pettigrew, this is carrying professional detachment too far. How can he expect me to interest myself in his twopenny halfpenny report at a moment like this? However, to humour him, he said, 'It is certainly very annoying for you. I appreciate that. I suppose you haven't kept a copy, and this means the loss of a good many days' hard work?'

Mallett opened the little despatch case he had brought with him, and produced from it some twenty sheets of typed paper, pinned together.

'Naturally, I have a copy, sir,' he said. 'I can hardly expect you to read it all now, but I'd just like you to cast your eye over' – he flicked over a number of sheets – 'pages 8 and 9, if you wouldn't mind. Then perhaps you will follow what I mean when I refer to the loss of the original as serious.'

Pettigrew unwillingly set to work to read the rather blurred carbon copy which Mallett put before him. His mind still running on Miss Danville, the words under his eyes seemed at first completely meaningless, and he had to read the first sentences two or three times before they conveyed any sense to him. Then, with an effort, he focused his attention on the pages and read them through with care.

'It occurs to me,' he said when he had finished, 'that what is exercising your mind, Inspector, is not so much the loss of your report as the possibility that someone may have found it.'

'Exactly, sir. As you will have seen, the report deals with what I may call the background of the Blenkinsop affair. In itself, that's a small matter – a quantity of stuff disposed of without licences, and at illegal prices. We shan't have any difficulty in proving our case, as I think you agree, and so far as it goes it will be a very useful little prosecution. But that isn't what I came up to Marsett Bay for. I'm concerned with a very wide-spread evasion of the Control, of which the Blenkinsop case is only one small instance. And it's an evasion that I'm convinced could only take place with connivance and assistance from inside. I won't bother you with the details, sir, they are all in the copy report you have there. But knowledge of the Control's methods of fighting the Black Market is getting outside.'

'And, to judge from the passage I have just read,' said Pettigrew, 'if this report gets into the wrong hands, a good deal more knowledge is going to get outside.'

'This report,' said Mallett seriously, 'contains a full statement of the whole case. It sets out all the evidence we have got so far, what evidence we are hoping to get in the future and how we mean to set about getting it. It gives our plan of campaign, suggestions for tightening up the security system inside the office and outside it – in fact, the whole works. If it has gone the wrong way, the case is as good as dead. I might as well go back to the Yard tomorrow and say the inquiry is a failure.'

'Unless you stayed up here to investigate Miss Danville's murder,' Pettigrew could not help saying.

Mallett smiled.

'I know what you're thinking, sir,' he said. 'You think this business is all very small beer compared to the other. And so it may be. You know how hard it is to feel enthusiastic about these war-time regulations. But I have my reputation to consider, whatever the nature of the inquiry may be.'

'At any rate, nobody can blame you for what has happened. That is, if it has happened. Aren't we rather jumping to conclusions, Inspector?'

'That brings me to the next point. We shall have to investigate now and see at what point the report may have gone astray. Do you mind if we have your secretary back for a moment?'

Pettigrew wearily agreed. Depressed and bewildered by the tragedy that had overtaken Miss Danville, he felt utterly uninterested in the fate of Mallett's report or the Blenkinsop prosecution or the black market in general. Still, it was a job that had to be done, and, unhappily, he appeared to be the man who must do it.

Miss Brown, when appealed to, was able to carry the matter a little further. The Controller's secretary had been very precise in detailing the movements of the papers up to the time they had left her. After the Controller had seen the report, she had taken it from his desk, addressed it to Pettigrew with an official label pinned securely to the front and left it in her 'Out' tray. From that tray, she had impressed on Miss Brown in a way that could leave no room for ambiguity, she had seen the messenger remove it, with a number of others – seen him, she had repeated more than once, with her own eyes.

'What time would this be?' Mallett asked.

'In the afternoon, when the messenger made his second round, she told me.'

'Then I can fix it,' said Pettigrew. 'It would be just before half-past three. I always hear him come down the corridor from the Controller's room about that time.'

'It should have reached you at half-past three, then?'

'No. For some reason, although he comes past my door at that time, he never delivers to me until some time later, usually about twenty past four, when I am just finishing my tea. It is only surmise on my part, but I have always imagined that it had some connexion with his own tea.'

'The next step, clearly, is to see the messenger. Where is he to be found?'

'There I'm afraid I can't help you,' said Pettigrew. 'It's remiss of me, perhaps, but the private life of messengers has always been a closed book to me. Perhaps it is because they always bring me such extremely tiresome stuff with them when they call that I have instinctively averted my eyes from the subject. Miss Brown, you have a much more practical mind than I. Where would you look for our man?'

Miss Brown looked at her watch.

'Just now,' she said with assurance, 'the messengers will be having their elevenses in the messengers' room. That's the little room on the landing half-way up the back stairs.'

'Marvellous! But I knew you could be depended on. Do you feel brave enough to penetrate to his lair and bring him down here?'

'Wait a minute,' said Mallett. 'I suppose these men

change their beats from day to day. How do we know which was on duty here on Friday?'

'That's all right. For once in a way, I did notice him yesterday. I had to get his assistance to open the door to the pantry where Miss Danville was. Of course, you haven't heard all the details of that matter, Inspector. But you saw him too, Miss Brown. A heavy, darkish man. Slow and dependable, I should say.'

'His name is John Peabody,' said Miss Brown. 'Shall I fetch him, Mr Pettigrew?'

After she had gone, Pettigrew remarked, 'A secretary who takes the trouble to find out even the messengers' christian names is a bit out of the ordinary, Inspector.'

'I'm prepared to believe that she's not very likely to lose important papers, at any rate,' was Mallett's comment.

John Peabody, when he appeared a few minutes later, was evidently not too pleased at being called from his refreshment to answer an enquiry into a missing document. In any event, he pointed out, there was a recognized procedure to be followed when any papers had gone astray. It involved, to begin with, filling up a form in triplicate, one copy of which went to the Registry, one to the head messenger, and the third to the branch originating the missing file. After that, the next step was. . . .

'I'm afraid we haven't time for all that in this case,' said Mallett.

'It doesn't say anything about time in the regulations,' Peabody replied severely.

'Perhaps I ought to explain,' said Pettigrew, 'that this gentleman is from Scotland Yard ― ―'

'Ah!' Peabody was visibly impressed.

'Special Branch,' he added quite untruthfully.

'Oh! Pleased to meet you, sir!'

'So you can understand we want to fill up as few of these forms and things as possible.'

Peabody pursed his lips and nodded wisely.

'What do you want to know, gents?' he said.

'The missing papers,' said Mallett, 'were taken by you from the Controller's secretary's room on Friday afternoon. That would be about half-past three?'

'That's right.'

'What did you do with them?'

'The usual.'

'What is that?'

'Put 'em on the shelf while I went for me tea.'

'The shelf? What's that?'

'Well, it's a shelf, so to speak. In the corridor here, just beyond this door.'

'Do you always do that with papers at this time of day?'

'Yes.'

'Why?'

'So's not to have to take 'em upstairs to me tea and down again, of course.'

'Do the other messengers follow the same procedure as you when they are on this beat?'

'Any that have any sense do.'

'Very good. Then after tea you came downstairs, went to the shelf, and found the papers had gone?'

'Wrong both times,' said Peabody with great satisfaction. 'After me tea I come down the back stairs and go through half a dozen rooms emptying their 'Out' trays, till I gets back here. Then I pick up off the shelf and back I go delivering, see? As for finding the papers gone, I never did any such thing. I dare say there was half a dozen bundles I laid down there, and how was I to tell if there was only five when I comes to pick them up again?'

'Are you sure this was what you did on Friday?'

'Yes. Why not?'

'But Friday was rather an unusual day, wasn't it?'

'I don't think so.'

'Well, it isn't every day you find ladies dying in the pantry, surely?'

Peabody sucked his teeth reflectively.

'That's so,' he admitted. 'I dare say that little business may have made me as much as half a minute late on my round, not more. As soon as I saw the lady was gone, I just carried on as usual. It was none of my business, anyway.'

'I see. Are there any questions you want to ask, Mr Pettigrew?'

'No, I don't think so.'

'Thank you, Peabody. That is all.'

'Thank you, sir.'

'Well,' said Mallett, after Peabody had retired to finish his elevenses, 'it seems clear enough how the papers could have disappeared. For about three-quarters of an hour they were lying outside there on the shelf for anybody who chose to lift them.'

'It sounds simple enough,' said Pettigrew, stifling a yawn.

'Anybody who chose,' the inspector repeated slowly. 'That implies a good deal, when you come to look at it. It isn't everybody who would choose, is it?'

'Obviously not,' said Pettigrew, beginning to feel like a participant in one of Plato's dialogues when Socrates really got going.

'Somebody,' Mallett went on remorselessly, 'who knew what to look for. Somebody who was expecting this very document, or something like it. That means, somebody who knew what was going on in this case already. Have you lost any other papers since you've been here, sir?'

'No. I often wished I could, but not one has managed to escape before. But – –'

'But what?'

'Three-quarters of an hour is ample time in which to prig a few papers, skim through them, even copy the parts that interest you most, and replace them.'

'If,' Mallett put in, 'if the individual had taken the trouble to ascertain beforehand exactly what the messenger's movements were. And – –'

'By Jove!'

'Yes, Mr Pettigrew?'

'Only something that has just struck me. But go on with what you were saying.'

'I was going to say: Why take the risk of stealing this report, which was bound to be found out, instead of just reading it and replacing it, if there was all that time to spare?'

'Because on Friday there wasn't time to spare,' said Pettigrew, now beginning for the first time to show some animation. 'Because on Friday, before the messenger came back on his round, there was Miss Danville in the room next door – –'

'Wasn't she always there about the same time?'

'Yes, yes, but she was deaf anyway. She doesn't count. But this time, there was also Miss Brown and Mrs Hopkinson and myself, trying to get in.'

'Somebody else, too, before that,' observed Mallett very quietly.

'Somebody else? I don't quite follow.'

'Unless, of course, either you or Miss Brown or Mrs Hopkinson stabbed Miss Danville.'

'Good God, yes! For the moment I had forgotten. The whole thing fits in. . . . Look here, Inspector, you've simply got to take up the Danville case now!'

'It's certainly beginning to look like it,' said the inspector. He did not seem at all unhappy at the prospect.

'Of course,' Pettigrew went on, 'the person who pinched your report may have been the same person who killed Miss Danville.'

'That is a possibility. But aren't we running on a little too fast? Where I should like your assistance, sir, is in trying to determine who that somebody we spoke of just now could be. This is a fairly quiet corridor as a rule, isn't it? You should know who is normally about this part of the building in the afternoon and who not. Have you noticed anything——'

'Stop, stop, Inspector! Give me a moment to collect my thoughts and I will answer all your questions and several you haven't asked yet. I'm beginning to understand quite a lot of things about this madhouse which I never did before. Now, listen and I will a tale unfold that. . . . No, Miss Brown, I am not going to sign those letters now. I don't care if they miss the midday post or not. I'm busy. And I shall not answer the telephone, not for the Lord Chancellor himself. . . . No, I am not expecting him to ring me up, but in case he should. . . . Please, *please*, Miss Brown, go away! . . . Now, Inspector, just see what you can make of this. . . .'

'Excuse me, Mr Pettigrew,' said Miss Brown, a quarter of an hour later.

'Miss Brown, I said I was *busy*!'

'I know, but I think you should see this. It seems to be important.'

'Very well then, put it down on the side table, and I'll attend to it directly. . . . What is it, anyway?'

'The Inspector's report about Blenkinsop, Mr Pettigrew. It came in just now, by the midday messenger.'

# CHAPTER TWELVE

## *The Inquest and After*

MALLETT looked with an impassive face at the document which Miss Brown had laid on the table. Neither he nor Pettigrew said anything for a moment or two. Then he rose to his feet, rather wearily.

'Well,' he said, 'it is what one might expect, isn't it? Borrowed and returned. I'm only surprised it hasn't got the usual Civil Service minute, "Seen, thank you", at the end. I don't suppose the messenger has the slightest idea where he picked it up, either. He just found it in someone's tray along with a lot of other stuff and brought it along in the ordinary way. And if I hadn't happened to come in this morning, there'd have been nothing whatever to show that it hadn't come here straight from the Controller's room.'

'It makes me wonder how many of my other files have taken the same trip,' said Pettigrew.

'I don't suppose we shall ever know that. I blame myself for ever letting the report leave my hands, but it's too late to think about that. Well, it all fits in, doesn't it, Mr Pettigrew? We've had a very interesting talk, anyway, and I shan't forget what you have told me. I'll see you at the inquest this afternoon.'

The inquest was sparsely attended. Besides Pettigrew, the only member of the Control who was present was the Establishment Officer, who presumably had come to ascertain where and by what means his establishment had been reduced by one. The local press was represented by an untidy young woman, from whose lacklustre expression it was easy to see that no advance information of the morning's discovery had been allowed to leak out. A jury of seven looked as wooden as juries do all the world over. Apart from these, there were not a dozen people in court, and nobody who had not noticed that at least half of them were plain clothes policemen would have guessed that the proceedings would be of the smallest interest.

A troubled-looking middle-aged man with a black tie was the first witness. He proved to be Miss Danville's brother and only near relation. He gave evidence of identifying his sister's body in the hospital mortuary and disappeared from the witness-box in a matter of seconds. The untidy young woman jotted down a few words, tapped her pencil against her teeth and yawned. She was still yawning when the doctor whom Pettigrew remembered from Friday afternoon briefly described being called to the offices of the Pin Control and finding Miss Danville already dead. Then the county pathologist came into the box to detail the result of his post-mortem examination. It was couched in language of the severest technicality and it was an appreciable time before the reporter realized its purport. Then she began to scribble furiously.

In plain English, Miss Danville had died from a stab wound in the abdomen. The wound was very small and very deep. It had penetrated the renal artery and caused internal haemorrhage which might be expected to produce death in a matter of minutes. The weapon used was evidently long, rigid, thin, and sharply pointed. It was certainly not a knife of the ordinary type. Rather, the pathologist suggested, a stiletto. The edges of the wound were not incised. It was a puncture wound, indicating that, apart from the sharp point, the instrument was cylindrical in shape. If he might hazard a guess — But the coroner was not encouraging guessing, and the witness passed on to an elaborate but irrelevant description of every other part of Miss Danville's anatomy, none of which showed any particular signs of abnormality. Pettigrew, who knew nothing of medicine, was interested to note that her poor, muddled wits had apparently inhabited a physically unimpaired brain. There were, the pathologist concluded, no other traces of injury.

As Mallett had predicted, at this point the coroner formally adjourned the inquest. While he was explaining to the jury that their duties were for the time being at an end, Pettigrew sat in a daze. He had known in advance what the gist of the pathologist's evidence would be, but none the less it had come as a shock to him. He tried to picture that small, deep, punctured wound. 'If I might hazard a guess,' he repeated to himself. It would have been interesting to know what the fellow was going to say. Not that it mattered. He could guess better for himself. He felt as if he had known it all along. What was it Edelman had said? 'We have fixed everything, even to the weapon. . . . Known locally as bodkins.' All part of what Mrs Hopkinson called 'the giddy Plot'! And now in some nightmare fashion the plot had come alive, the silly farce turned itself into grim tragedy. For a moment he thought he was going to be sick. Then he came to himself and realized that everyone in court was standing up, and that Inspector Jellaby was beckoning him.

Pettigrew meekly followed him to the police-station. Mallett, who had occupied an inconspicuous seat at the back of the court, had preceded them and was already in Jellaby's office when they arrived. Here, also, he seemed determined to make himself as small as it was physically possible for him to do, and for the first part of the long interview that followed remained seated quietly in a corner, idly watching the smoke curling upwards from his pipe.

At Jellaby's request, Pettigrew went through in detail all that he could remember of the events of Friday afternoon. It was little enough that he had to tell, and in retrospect he could think of nothing that could at the time have led him to suspect that Miss Danville's death was a violent one.

'You saw nothing that might have been used as a weapon?' Jellaby asked.

'No. I wasn't looking for anything, of course. But the room was small and pretty bare.'

'And since then there have been three days to clear it up in,' said Jellaby bitterly. 'Still, it must have been a fairly unusual kind of instrument.'

'There are plenty of them about in the Control,' said Pettigrew. 'I think my secretary has one.'

'What are you speaking about, sir?'

'Sharp, pointed instruments. Known locally as bodkins. They are used for piercing holes in bundles of papers for filing.'

'And why are you so certain that was what was used in this case?'

'This,' said Pettigrew wearily, 'is going to take rather a lot of explaining.'

'Would it be connected with what was known as the Plot, sir?'

'Oh, you've heard about that, have you?'

'Mr Mallett has given me a few notes of what you told him this morning, and perhaps it will save you some trouble if I just run through them with you now.'

He pulled from a drawer in his desk some closely written sheets of paper and from them read an amazingly accurate *résumé* of the conversation of the morning. Glancing across to Mallett, Pettigrew fancied that he could detect on that broad, good-humoured face a subdued glow of self-satisfaction as the recital proceeded. He had taken no notes of the interview and the exactitude of its reproduction was a sample of the phenomenal memory on which he prided himself.

'Well, sir,' said Jellaby, as he finished reading, 'does that statement cover your experiences since you have been at Marsett Bay, so far as this case is concerned?'

'Not altogether. You must remember that I was primarily concerned with the inquiry into the Blenkinsop affair, and all that that entails. Also, I hadn't then heard the evidence at the inquest.'

'That brings us to what you were telling us just now, sir. Where do the bodkins come into it?'

Pettigrew repeated what he could remember of the conversation with Edelman that had haunted his mind ever since he had heard the pathologist's evidence.

'I didn't mention it to Inspector Mallett this morning,' he added. 'I couldn't see that it was relevant.'

'Doesn't make sense,' said Jellaby shortly.

'I know,' said Pettigrew faintly. 'It doesn't make sense that Edelman should advertise to me in advance the means by which he intended to commit a murder. It doesn't make sense that he should want to kill Miss Danville, anyway. I don't say for a moment that he did. Yet I feel positive that whoever did it used that very weapon. You can ask the pathologist about that. But does anything in this case make sense? Why should anyone want to kill Miss Danville, of all people?'

Inspector Jellaby made no reply. His expression said plainly enough that he regarded it as his function to ask questions rather than to answer them.

'Is there anything else you can tell us, Mr Pettigrew?' he went on.

'Only this. When I spoke to Miss Danville at lunch on the day that she died, I got the very clear impression that she was trying to tell me something.'

'You have told us that already, sir.'

'Yes, but what I want to make clear is this. The reason why I refused to listen to her – and I shall never forgive myself for it – was that I took it for granted that she was simply wanting to do what she had already tried to do the previous evening – explain her outburst at the Fernlea Club, which, of course, was simply part of her sad mental history. But looking back on it now, I feel sure that she really had something important to tell me. And if that is right, it must have been something that had happened or that she had got to know during that morning. It's a point that might be worth following up.'

'I see,' said Jellaby doubtfully. He wrote down a few notes and then sat silent. The interview seemed to be at an end, or at all events at a standstill. Then Mallett took his pipe out of his mouth, cleared his throat, and said in an almost deprecatory tone, 'There are just one or two points that occur to me. For one thing, I am rather interested in this locked door. The door of the room where she was found, I mean. The messenger opened it, didn't he?'

'Yes.'

'Was there usually a key in the lock of that door?'

'I'm afraid I have no idea.'

'We've all been assuming – at least, I have – that it had been locked from the outside. But could it have been done from within? What about the window? Was it open?'

'Certainly not wide open. I have a vague idea it wasn't completely closed, but I can't be sure.'

Mallett clicked his tongue against his teeth. 'And all

this happened three days ago, so now there's no possible means of knowing. Now, another thing,' he went on. 'Before the Thursday evening, did anybody at the Fern-lea Club know that Miss Danville had been in a mental hospital?'

'So far as I can tell, no. It was common knowledge that she was somewhat abnormal in some ways. Wood was the first person to spot it, I remember. I suppose his training as a novelist would make him exceptionally alive to that sort of thing. But I think I can say the fact came as a surprise to everyone in the room.'

'And everyone in the room at the time was on more or less bad terms with her?'

'I should hardly put it that way, Inspector, because that implies some reciprocity, and you couldn't say that Miss Danville ever showed up to that evening that she was much affected by what other people thought of her. But it is true to say that the only people, myself apart, who didn't dislike her in one way or another were Phillips and Miss Brown. Miss Brown, of course, was away on leave on this particular evening.'

'Which of them would you say showed the greatest enmity towards her?'

'That's a very difficult question to answer. I should think the word "enmity" much too strong in every case, if by that you mean a feeling powerful enough to induce a motive for murder. So far as my opinion is worth anything, it is that everyone concerned had a different attitude towards her. Miss Clarke, for example, regarded her just as a blot on the landscape from the official point of view. She wasn't much use in the department, and Miss Clarke doesn't suffer fools gladly. Mrs Hopkinson was a good deal more personal in the matter. She seemed to feel rather bitterly towards her, because of the encouragement she had been giving to Phillips and my secretary. Whether it was, as she represented to me, because she thought Miss Brown was throwing herself away or because of some more personal reason, I couldn't say.'

'Mrs Hopkinson's real enmity was towards Mr Phillips, was it not?'

'Apparently so. Indeed, the trouble on Thursday night began from her taking the opportunity of Phillips being out of the room to slander him behind his back. She had got it into her head that he was a potential bigamist, and told poor Miss Danville such a circumstantial story that she was thoroughly upset. If it hadn't been for that, I don't think she would have broken down as she did later on.'

'I don't think you mentioned this to me, this morning, sir,' said Mallett reproachfully.

'I'm sorry, but it seemed quite irrelevant. It still does, for the matter of that, but you are the best judges of what is important and what isn't.'

'Anything may be important at this stage,' said Jellaby. 'So she thought Mr Phillips had a wife alive, did she?'

'A wife and several children, to be accurate.'

'What should make her say that?'

'Pure spite, I imagine. There was not a word of truth in it, of course.'

'And how do you know that?'

'I don't know how Mr Pettigrew knows it,' said Mallett, 'but he is right about Mr Phillips being a widower. I have seen Mrs Phillips's death certificate.'

Pettigrew looked at him in surprise.

'Why on earth, Inspector?' he asked.

'Routine,' Mallett answered. 'I told you I have made a study of a number of the employees in the Control for my own inquiry, and I naturally checked up on their personal histories. I believe in thoroughness in these matters.'

'Well,' said Pettigrew, 'I didn't go quite as far as you, but for my own purposes' – he flushed uncomfortably – 'that is to say, because I felt a certain responsibility towards Miss Brown, I had made inquiries through other channels, with, of course, the same result. Consequently, I was able to stifle Mrs Hopkinson and reassure Miss Danville.'

'Was that a great relief to her?' Mallett asked.

'Very much so. In fact, she burst into tears, and had to leave the room. It was most embarrassing. She came back just in time for Rickaby to precipitate her final breakdown. You know of that already.'

'So much for Mrs Hopkinson. I'm afraid she's been the cause of rather a digression. You were describing the attitude of the residents to Miss Danville, and there are still the men to deal with.'

'Well, Rickaby thought her extremely funny. He is the type of gentleman who thinks that if there is one thing in nature more inherently amusing than an old maid it is a lunatic, and when the two are combined the joke is, of course, irresistible. I thought we had grown out of such things nowadays, but apparently I was wrong. Edelman can hardly be said to have shown dislike to her at all. But then he is not the type to show his feelings, anyway. He regarded her as an interesting psychological specimen and I think he was quite prepared to cause her any amount of pain just to observe her reactions. When I say pain, I don't of course mean – –'

'I quite understand, sir. Please go on.'

'Well, that only leaves Wood and Phillips. Phillips, as I have said, was to all appearances fond of her – as he ought to have been in all conscience, for I don't think he'd have made much headway with Miss Brown without her. Wood seemed to consider her principally as a potential subject for a story, and if he disliked her, as I think he did, it was probably mainly on the score that she disapproved of him and his works. I'm afraid I've put all this very crudely,' Pettigrew concluded. 'But what I find very difficult to convey is the atmosphere at the Fernlea. There was definitely an anti-Danville party, although all the members of it arrived at their position in different ways. But I should have thought the last thing any of them would have wanted was to murder the poor woman.'

'Motive known – none,' muttered Jellaby, writing as he spoke. 'Next stage – opportunity.'

'This is where my own inquiry may be of some help,' observed Mallett. 'It seems to me that the person who had the opportunity of intercepting my report on its way from Mr Palafox to Mr Pettigrew had also an opportunity to kill Miss Danville. The two things must have happened within a few yards of each other and within a very short space of time.'

'Doesn't follow the same person did both,' Jellaby objected.

'Certainly not, although it is possible, and if so, perhaps it would shed some light on the motive. I think that the interests we are fighting would be prepared to use pretty drastic methods to prevent us exposing their means of breaking the control. But that isn't my point. What I mean is that the same group of people fall under suspicion in each case as being likely to be on the spot at the right time. Now to begin with, Mr Pettigrew, I am right in thinking that nobody, apart from the messenger, would normally have had any business there at that hour of the day?'

'So far as my knowledge of the office routine goes, no.'

'Except Mr Pettigrew and Miss Brown,' said Jellaby.

'I apologize,' said Pettigrew. 'I was forgetting that so far as opportunity goes, ours was as good as, or indeed better than, anyone's. It would be a little embarrassing to us all to discuss my own case, particularly as you haven't administered a caution yet; but I am quite prepared to answer for Miss Brown.'

'Perhaps you'd better. I'll be seeing her anyway,' Jellaby said with what seemed to Pettigrew unnecessary grimness.

'Well, to begin with, Miss Brown was actually with me when — No, that's wrong, I was forgetting.' He stopped, confused, and angry with himself for being confused. 'Let me get this right. First I heard the kettle starting to whistle. Then I heard what I took to be Miss Danville going to make the tea. The kettle went on whistling, and so when Miss Brown came into my room, I naturally assumed that it was her footsteps I had heard and not Miss Danville's. I know now of course that my first supposition was right.'

'Do you?' said Jellaby.

'Well — dash it, Miss Danville *was* there. We know that now.'

'And where was Miss Brown?'

'I — I really have no idea, except that she came into my room while the kettle was whistling and I sent her to turn it off. She may have been in her room some time, of course, long enough to take off her hat and coat, anyway.'

'You didn't hear her come into her room?'

'No. I wasn't listening for her, naturally. I didn't expect her at all that day. And she has very light footsteps anyway.'

'Rubber-soled shoes, perhaps?'

'I dare say. I have never troubled to find out.'

'And coming into the building by the ordinary entrance she would have to pass the scene of the crime to reach her room?'

'Really,' said Pettigrew warmly, 'I must protest. It is a ridiculous notion that Miss Brown could conceivably be guilty of an act of violence against anyone, let alone Miss Danville. It simply outrages reason to suggest that a girl like that – –'

'Well, well,' Mallett interposed tactfully. 'Suppose we go back to where I started just now. Apart from you two and the messenger, there was nobody who ought to have been in that vicinity at that time?'

Pettigrew, who was conscious of having made himself look rather foolish by his over-emphatic advocacy on his secretary's behalf, considered the question as coolly as possible before replying.

'There are two possibilities which have just occurred to me,' he said. 'One is that the Controller might have sent for some member of the staff who would normally take that route to his room. You can easily ascertain whether that happened on this occasion, of course.'

'Good. That point will be attended to. And the other possibility?'

'Next to the pantry where Miss Danville died, and on the side farthest from my room, is a ladies' cloakroom. That means of course that any woman working in that part of the building might properly be within quite a short distance of the pantry door at any time.'

'Thank you, sir. It looks as if a lot of ladies will have to be asked about their visits to that room on Friday afternoon. Well, that covers authorized persons. Now for the unauthorized. You had at different times had to suffer from the presence of intruders in your corridor?'

'Edelman, Wood, Hopkinson, Rickaby, Phillips,' Jellaby enumerated, reading from Mallett's notes.

'That is right. But I don't want to mislead you about this. I was several times aware of people fooling about outside my door, and on each occasion it was in the afternoon and about the time we are considering in this case – between half-past three and four. The only time I caught them in the act it proved to be Edelman, Wood, and Mrs Hopkinson. It doesn't prove, of course, that it was the same three, or any of them, on the previous occasions. Phillips I found on the same day' – the recollection of the circumstances still made him feel uncomfortable – 'but it was a good deal later, after tea. Rickaby was earlier, about one o'clock. And in both the last two cases, there was a perfectly reasonable explanation for their presence.'

'The explanation of the others did not strike you as so reasonable,' Mallett commented.

'No, it didn't.'

'You told me a very odd story this morning, sir, about what became known as the Plot. What is your candid opinion of it?'

Pettigrew shrugged his shoulders.

'I gave up trying to form an opinion of it some time ago,' he said. 'Except that it was a damned nuisance. It started as a quite amusing game, and seems to have ended as an obsession.'

'You didn't think there was anything behind it?'

'Behind it?'

'Some ulterior motive on the part of the plotters?'

'I can't say I did. The whole thing seemed to me completely purposeless and silly.'

'Purposeless or not,' interrupted Jellaby. 'Look at the results.'

'Surely,' Pettigrew objected, 'you can't say that anything that happened was a result of the Plot. At least, you can't prove it at this stage.'

'I never heard of the Plot till I read these notes over my lunch,' said Jellaby, 'but I've found two results already. Miss Danville driven off her head – I call that one result. The other one is that all the plotters knew exactly what to expect in this part of the building at the exact time of the crime. Knowledge on the part of suspects – I call that another result, and maybe the bigger one of the two.'

'There were only three present at the rehearsal which I interrupted,' said Pettigrew.

'They were all in the room plotting it out together on the Thursday evening, or so you told Mr Mallett this morning.'

Pettigrew disliked Jellaby's uncompromising methods of argument, but he was compelled to admit that he was right. Still he remained unconvinced on the main issue.

'It seems to me difficult to believe that such an elaborate pretence should have been built up over such a long period without anyone giving it away,' he said.

'The secret – if there was a secret – needn't have been known to all of them,' Mallett pointed out. 'Possibly the Plot came into existence quite accidentally, and then one or more of the plotters decided to make use of it as a convenient cover for other activities. But we're straying into theory. At present, we do possess the two solid results of the Plot mentioned by Mr Jellaby just now. How they fit into the rest of the story we don't know yet, but I think it's asking rather a lot to believe that neither of them have anything to do with either my inquiry or Mr Jellaby's. Is there anything further you would like to tell us, sir?'

'Nothing,' said Pettigrew, and rose to go.

'Good afternoon, sir. By the way, I have just heard

from London that summonses are being issued against Blenkinsops under Article 7 (1) (d) of the Order, just as you advised.'

'That is a tremendous consolation, isn't it?' said Pettigrew.

# CHAPTER THIRTEEN

## Talking About It

'This fellow,' observed Mallett to Jellaby, as he entered the latter's office next morning, 'really had the most astonishing luck.'

Jellaby looked up from his desk, on which were laid the first fruits of his inquiry, a set of photographs of the scene of Miss Danville's death, and another of the body of the lady herself.

'What fellow?' he asked absently.

'Our murderer, of course – or murderess, as the case may be.'

Jellaby grunted and resumed his study of the photographs.

'Ought to be a close-up of the window,' he murmured. Then he looked up suddenly. 'Did you say *our* murderer?' he asked.

Mallett nodded. 'Ours now,' he said. 'It came through to my digs just after breakfast. Your chief must have been pretty emphatic on the telephone yesterday evening to get it arranged so quickly. I am to be in charge of this investigation, subject to my continuing to do what I can in the Blenkinsop affair – which is pretty well cleaned up, anyway – and the enquiry into the leakage of information from the Control. That's an affair I have very small hopes of now, unless this one throws some light on it. So there we are. I hope you have no objections.'

'Objections? No. Glad to have you. Don't care for Yard men butting in as a rule, but this is different. Not a local business, properly speaking. All foreigners involved. You'll understand 'em better than I should.'

'I'm glad you feel that way about it,' said Mallett. 'I hoped you would.'

'Matter of fact,' Jellaby grunted, rather as though a confession was being forced from him, 'matter of fact, I asked for you myself. Well,' he went on hastily, before Mallett could thank him, 'you'll want to see what I've got so far. Haven't had much time since our talk with Mr Pettigrew yesterday, but such as it is, it's here.'

Mallett drew up a chair to the desk and read with concentrated attention the papers which Jellaby placed before him. At the end of ten minutes, he pushed his chair back and lighted his pipe.

'Well, you've cleared the ground a bit, Mr Jellaby,' he observed. 'Let's summarize what you've got here. Statement from Establishment Officer – pure routine, and nothing of any value in it. Statement from her brother: his sister had no enemies that he knew of; she had suffered from melancholia in the past, but had been apparently cured several years ago; no suicidal tendencies, so far as he is aware. Well, this isn't a case of suicide, we can bank on that. It doesn't look like a self-inflicted wound anyhow, and apart from that, if she killed herself, how did she manage to dispose of the weapon? Statement from the pathologist: The wound is certainly consistent with the use of a paper piercer of the type now produced and shown to him. That's one up to Mr Pettigrew, anyway. Statement from Miss Hawker, assistant principal in charge of the Stationery Department at the Control: Eighty-seven paper piercers (known colloquially as "bodkins"), large, have been issued for the use of the officers of the Pin Control; these are distributed according to demand among all the sections in the office; number now accounted for, sixty-eight; it is against the rules to remove these for personal use, but she fears it is done. It doesn't look as if we shall get very far in that direction. Now if Miss Clarke had been in charge of the Stationery Department, I don't expect a single paper clip could have been moved from one room to another without a requisition form in triplicate. What's next? This is interesting – Statement from John Peabody, messenger: Further to previous statement, he adds that, according to usual routine, after depositing his papers on the shelf and before proceeding upstairs to his tea, he went into the pantry, filled the kettle and lighted the gas-ring; the room was then empty, and he observed nothing and nobody suspicious. Lastly, Statement from Elizabeth Evans, landlady of the Fernlea Residential Club: At the request of Detective-Inspector Jellaby, she now hands to him all books, papers, and documents in the room lately occupied by Honoria Danville, deceased – which have not been disturbed in any way since her death. What about the books and documents, Mr Jellaby. Is there anything of interest there?'

'Nothing at all. They're all here if you want to look at 'em, but you'd be wasting your time. Very few letters, and they were of no consequence. There was a fattish note-book, labelled "Journal", which I had hopes of. But there was nothing in it but prayers and so forth. I didn't like it at all, I can tell you, though I thought it my duty to read every word of it. Nasty stuff. Very high, she must have been. Very high indeed – almost Romish. I'm a Free Churchman myself.'

'Well,' said Mallett, 'you've certainly wasted no time up to date. But I'm afraid we're going to have our work cut out to make up the three days we lost before we ever began.'

'That's true. As you said just now, this chap's had the

devil's own luck. Could hardly have relied on getting away with a start like that, could he?'

'No,' Mallett agreed. 'And I think that's rather an important point. Because, assuming, as he must have assumed, that the murder was going to be discovered as soon as anyone went into the room, he was obviously taking a tremendous risk. At the most, he could only count on a few minutes to make his getaway. The fact that there was only one wound, which he couldn't have been sure would be fatal, shows what a hurry he was in. Every murder is a risk, of course, but anyone planning in advance to dispose of Miss Danville could, I should have thought, have devised something with a greater margin of safety. Why was it done this way, then?'

'Unpremeditated attack, perhaps,' suggested Jellaby. 'Sudden quarrel and a flare-up – like nine murders out of ten are, anyhow.'

'A sudden quarrel with a deafish woman in a room with all that row going on from the kettle? It doesn't seem very plausible to me.'

'Sudden emergency, then.'

'That's what I'm looking for. I think it looks as though he (and in "he" I'm always including "she", of course) took his quick opportunity to get rid of Miss Danville because he had to. In other words, something had happened, or was just going to happen, which made it urgently necessary for him to kill her.'

'Such as – – ?'

Mallett left the question in the air while he knocked out his pipe.

'One could imagine half a dozen situations in which the removal of someone might become suddenly necessary,' he said, 'but I don't think there's much to be gained by starting from that point. I'd rather begin at the other end – which was where the murderer began, after all, with Miss Danville. What are the salient facts about her, and what new development, if any, had recently occurred with regard to those facts? If we examine those, we may get a clue to what was in our fellow's mind.'

'First salient fact,' said Jellaby. 'She was mad.'

'Yes, that certainly leaps to the eye as the most important thing about her. Not that she was mad in the ordinary sense of the term – I don't suppose any doctor would have certified her. But she was unquestionably abnormal in some ways.'

'She had been in an asylum, hadn't she?'

'Yes, but as a voluntary patient only. I checked that up when I was looking into the antecedents of the Fernlea crowd. Even the Government in war-time would hardly have given her a job if she had actually been certified insane. Well, that's our first point, I don't know that it carries us much further. As Mr Wood seemed to think, madness may be a good reason for committing a murder, but I don't see that it provides a motive for anyone else to kill the mad person – unless the insanity is of a very different type from Miss Danville's.

'But it is interesting to note that there had been a recent development affecting her mental condition, or rather two, one on top of the other. Firstly, the night before her death she had had what seems to have been a bad, though temporary, mental breakdown, and secondly, as a result of that, she had published the fact of having been in a mental hospital.'

'Second salient fact,' Jellaby went on, 'and the only other one that I can see is – a lot of people disliked her.'

'M'm,' said Mallett doubtfully, 'I'd rather prefer to split that one up. It's a bit broad for our purposes. Besides, it's the facts behind the dislike I want to look at. Shortly, I can see only two of substance. One is that she wanted Miss Brown to marry this man Phillips.'

'Nothing occurred lately to affect that,' said Jellaby.

'No, unless you count the fact that Miss Clarke and Mrs Hopkinson had publicly quarrelled with her the night before on that subject.'

'Miss Brown had just come back from London when the murder took place,' Jellaby observed. 'Could that possibly affect the position in any way?'

'Until we interview Miss Brown we can't answer that one,' Mallett replied. 'It is a possibility, of course, but it doesn't seem likely.'

'The other cause for dislike,' said Jellaby, 'was her objection to the Plot, or whatever they called the silly thing.'

'Exactly. And the recent development affecting that fact was that Rickaby disclosed that she had been cast for the part of the villain in the Plot.'

Jellaby, while Mallett was speaking, had been writing busily.

'I believe in making notes,' he explained. 'Helps to clear the mind sometimes. Care to see them?'

Mallett read the notes, which were as follows:

### MISS DANVILLE

1. Madness. *Developments:* (*a*) Breakdown. (*b*) Asylum revelation.

2. Encouraged Miss B.'s affair with P. *Developments:* (*a*) Attack from Miss C. and Mrs H. (*b*) Miss B.'s return from London (?).

3. Disapproval of Plot. *Development:* Told of part in ditto by R.

'It's certainly terse enough,' said Mallett, handing it back with a smile.

'All there, isn't it? I hate wordy stuff. Only fogs the mind.'

'Yes, it's all there. And you will note that every person whom Mr Pettigrew mentioned as having been near the scene of the crime at the time figures in it in one way or another.'

'Except Mr Pettigrew himself.'

'Yes, there is that one exception. And now that it's down in black and white, what does it suggest to you?'

'Nothing at all,' said Jellaby promptly.

Mallett took the sheet of notes again and stared at them, tugging his moustache the while.

'She was mad,' he said to himself. 'Everyone suspected that, it seems. *But* she had a breakdown on Thursday night *and* she gave away that she had been in an asylum. *Therefore* she had to be killed, in a hurry, on Friday. It doesn't make sense to me. Why had it suddenly become necessary to kill her because she made a scene in the Fernlea lounge or because she had let out her past history? Try again. She encouraged Miss Brown to accept Phillips. That, too, seems to have been notorious for a long time past. *But* Mrs Hopkinson took it into her head to blow her up publicly for it. Therefore—No, that's plain nonsense. Nobody was ever killed for having been abused in public. *But,* also, Miss Brown had just come back from London. I don't see that can be of any importance. Suppose while she was away Miss Brown had decided not to have him after all – as the result of having found out something against him, let us say. . . . Well, she would hardly go and kill her simply for giving her bad advice. And in that case, nobody else would have any motive left, if stopping the marriage was a motive. . . . I'm afraid I'm being very wordy,' Mallett added apologetically.

'That's all right,' Jellaby assured him. 'You're not fogging my mind – so far.'

'Good. Well, suppose Miss Brown came back meaning

to marry Phillips, she wouldn't have wanted to kill her main supporter, so we can count her out on that score. But how does it provide any sort of motive for anyone else? You don't prevent a marriage by eliminating the bridesmaid.'

'I don't think much of Salient Fact No. 2.'

'Is No. 3 any better? She disapproved of the Plot, and had shown her disapproval ever since it was first suggested. *But* she had just been told by one of the plotters that she had a part in the story, and that her function in it was to murder the Controller. This, coming on top of her scene with Mrs Hopkinson, sent her temporarily off her head. *Therefore,* it was necessary to remove her – why? Because she might have put a stop to this parlour game in some way? Or out of pique, because she wouldn't play?'

Jellaby shook his head.

'Look here, Mr Mallett,' he said, 'it's about time I reminded you that we're investigating the murder of a mad person and not looking for a mad murderer.'

'At least, we're not looking for a murderer who is obviously mad. And, so far as can be seen at present, none of the facts that we know about Miss Danville would provide any sane person with a motive for killing her, let alone a motive for killing her in a great hurry and at great risk.'

'I could have told you that before we started.'

Mallett laughed. 'I know what's in your mind,' he said, 'but all the same, I don't think we've wasted our time this morning. For one thing, we've assembled a highly unusual set of facts, and I think it's asking too much of coincidence to believe that they could all be present simultaneously and have nothing whatever to do with the fourth and most unusual fact of all, which is her murder. And, if we're right in thinking that the murder happened when it did because something had suddenly made it a matter of urgent necessity to the murderer, it is significant that in each case there had been a fresh development as recently as the preceding evening.'

'I'd like to find one that had happened as recently as Friday morning,' said Jellaby.

'Why so?'

'Don't you remember what Mr Pettigrew said? Miss Danville was trying to tell him something at lunch that day, and he wouldn't listen. He thought at the time it was only an explanation of her having come over queer the night before, but now he's sure it was something fresh.'

'He may be wrong there, of course. He is probably wrong about what she wanted to tell him the preceding night. There were two distinct stages, remember. First, Mr Pettigrew persuaded her that she need not believe Mrs Hopkinson's slanders about Phillips. She was so relieved that she started to cry and had to leave the room. When she came back, she was starting to make some sort of explanation, but Rickaby interrupted her. I don't see why she should have wished to tell him about her having been in an asylum before her final breakdown. Afterwards, she was in no shape to tell him anything. In any case, if something new did happen on Friday morning, we have no clue to it yet.'

'I was wondering,' Jellaby said. 'This Black Market business of yours. Could she have found out something, and wanted to tell him about it?'

'Hardly, I should think. It couldn't be the purloining of my report, anyway, because that couldn't have been till the afternoon. We'll check up her movements during that morning, so far as possible, to see if she had any opportunities of picking up information of that kind.'

'I think you raised the point earlier on,' Jellaby continued. 'Your report was lifted just about the time Miss Danville was killed. Can't tie it down to minutes, of course, but near enough the same time. Isn't it likely the same man did both? She caught him in the act. He killed her to stop her squealing. Nearest thing to a motive we've got so far, anyhow.'

'It looks feasible certainly, but the more I think about it, the less I like it. After all, the very last person to take a trespasser in the corridor by surprise would be Miss Danville. Her coming was always advertised beforehand by a steam whistle, which gave anyone ample time to get away. Besides, even if you can get over that difficulty, where did the bodkin come from, unless the murderer brought it with him, intending to use it? It's not the kind of thing you would normally want to walk about with, I should imagine. I think whoever killed Miss Danville went to the pantry for that specific purpose, and no other.'

The two men were silent for a moment or two. Inspector Jellaby drummed his knuckles on the edge of the desk, a habit of his when vexed or puzzled. Finally he said, somewhat tartly:

'It's getting clear to me that we're not going to make an arrest in this case by sitting here and talking about it!'

'I know,' said Mallett mildly. 'We've got to get busy now and take statements from everybody who can possibly throw any light on the affair. But before you start a search, it's a good thing to have some idea of what you're looking for. I think we know now what it is.'

'Do we? What is it, then?'

'A link. I want to find the link between one or more of our salient facts and this crime. On the face of it, there is no possible connexion between any of them and Miss

Danville's death, but I'm convinced there is one somewhere.'

'And what makes you say that?'

'Simply that if there is no connexion, the last two
days of Miss Danville's life were just an incoherent
jumble. I don't think things happen like that. There's
a pattern somewhere if we could only find the key to it.'

Jellaby sniffed.

'I was going to begin taking statements at the Control
this morning,' he said. 'You're in charge now, of course,
but – –'

'We'll go at once,' said Mallett.

# CHAPTER FOURTEEN

## Police Inquiries

From the police-station to the offices of the Pin Control was a quarter of an hour's walk. Mallett, brushing aside an offer of a police car, covered the distance in slightly less than ten minutes. Jellaby, panting beside him, was astonished how fit and active the bulky man proved to be. He had to save his breath for walking, and the journey was made in silence on his part. Such observations as Mallett threw out had no bearing on the matter in hand. Once within the grounds of the mansion, Mallett turned towards the side entrance.

'Where're we going?' Jellaby asked.

'I thought we must have a talk with Mr Palafox first. It seems only civil to start with the head of the department.'

'Can't just go bursting in on a man in his position, can we?' Jellaby objected. 'You're in charge, of course, but I'd have thought he'd want an appointment.'

'We have an appointment for eleven fifteen,' said Mallett. 'I arranged it this morning before I came round to see you. Sorry if I hurried you coming along, but I was afraid we'd be late.'

'And I thought you meant to stay gassing in my office all morning. Should have known better, I suppose.'

'I don't know why you should,' rejoined Mallett mildly, as they entered the side door. 'Good morning, Miss Unsworth!' he went on. 'Is the Controller ready to see us?'

Miss Unsworth, the Controller's secretary, gave the two men the malevolent look with which she always greeted anybody likely to trespass on her principal's time. But she had no excuse ready to put them off. The appointment had been made, and a glance at her watch told her that the visitors were neither too early nor too late for it. She had to content herself with saying sourly, 'Mr Palafox has a conference fixed for a quarter to twelve.'

'Oh, we shan't keep him nearly as long as that,' Mallett assured her, without producing any softening effect in her severe expression.

The detectives were ushered into the large, bare library, where, with his back firmly turned on the magnificent view over the bay, the Controller sat behind an enormous desk.

'This is Detective-Inspector Jellaby of the County Police, sir,' said Mallett.

'Just so,' said the Controller, vaguely. His voice was rich and plummy and he prided himself on the distinctness of his articulation. He waved Jellaby towards the less comfortable of the two chairs in front of the desk, and thereafter addressed himself exclusively to Mallett.

'I am very much concerned,' he went on, 'with the occurrence of last Friday.' He paused, to let the significance of his concern have its full weight. 'The loss of your report, Inspector, which has only recently been reported to me, is a development which I can only characterize as disturbing.'

'Quite so, sir.'

'It must of course, be recovered. I am sure I need not stress the importance of that.'

'It has been recovered, sir.'

'It has? But this is very surprising. When did this take place?'

'Yesterday.'

'How is it that this has not been reported to me?'

'I am afraid that I am to blame for that, sir. But both my colleague and I have been rather preoccupied with another inquiry since then.' Then, seeing the look of perplexity on the Controller's plump face, Mallett continued, 'I should explain that I have been put in charge of the investigation into the death of Miss Danville.'

'Miss Danville? The lady who – ? Yes, of course. Then that explains the presence of this gentleman here.' He indicated the speechless Jellaby, who was not accustomed to being treated as a piece of furniture in his own police division. 'But Inspector, am I then to understand that you have come here to interview me about a case of *murder*?'

'I think that you can be of some assistance to us, sir,' said Mallett deprecatingly. 'If only in a negative direction,' he added.

'In a negative direction – just so.' Mr Palafox had evidently decided that the situation called for a touch of humour. 'It is a process known in your profession as eliminating a suspect, is it not?'

'That isn't exactly what I had in mind, sir,' Mallett replied gravely. 'The purpose of my inquiry is this: I wish to establish, if possible, who might be expected to have been at or near the scene of Miss Danville's death at the critical time. Now the layout of this building is such that anyone coming towards this room from the main part of the office would have to pass the room where Miss Danville was found.'

'Or vice versa, Inspector, let me interpolate, or vice versa.'

'Exactly, sir. Now I take it that from time to time members of your staff do come to see you here?'

'Heads of departments naturally come to consult me occasionally; senior assistants less often, members of the staff of lower grades very rarely indeed. For ordinary purposes, in any case, I prefer to make use of the internal telephone system if it becomes necessary to discuss any point *viva voce*.'

'Very good, sir. Now on Friday last – –'

'You need not labour on your point, Inspector, I apprehended it some time ago. On Friday – but I will not trust my memory. Miss Unsworth will have a record of my engagements for that day and we will consult her.'

Miss Unsworth, when appealed to, produced the Controller's diary of engagements.

'Your only afternoon engagement on Friday,' she said, 'was at two-thirty. The Establishment Officer came to see you and brought Miss Clarke with him. They left at five minutes past three.'

'Just so. I recollect now, it was in relation to a rather awkward situation that had arisen with regard to Miss Danville. That reminds me, Miss Unsworth, you may cancel the memorandum I dictated on that subject. In view of what has since supervened it will not now be necessary. Thank you, Miss Unsworth. Does that meet your point, Inspector?'

'Perhaps Miss Unsworth can tell us whether anybody came to see Mr Palafox without an appointment that afternoon?'

'And failed to get past the Cerberus at the gate? That is always a possibility, is it not? Many call but few are chosen. What say you, Miss Unsworth?'

'There was nobody,' said Miss Unsworth drily. She looked again at the diary and added, 'From three-fifty-nine till four-five you were speaking on a call you had put through to London, and at four-ten a call came through from Birmingham, which you answered.'

'Thank you, Miss Unsworth. I am sure the Inspector

will take due note of the alibi you have so thoughtfully provided for me. I, on my side, can, I think, perform a like service for you. At both those times I heard your voice informing me that my connexion had been made, and in the interval I was aware of your typewriter functioning next door. Is that all, Inspector?'

It was Jellaby, tired of being ignored, who answered.

'This isn't the only room on this side of the building,' he said. 'There could have been visitors to them, I suppose?'

The Controller regarded him with the interest he might have accorded to a child who had made an unexpectedly clever remark in grown-up company.

'The point is well taken,' he said. 'But not, I fear, a good one. There are two other rooms besides mine at this end of the corridor. One belongs to the head of Export Control, Mr Bissett, and he, you will find, has been away on leave since Tuesday last. The other was until a fortnight ago in the occupation of a liaison officer from the Ministry of Manpower, when the Treasury in its wisdom decided that co-operation with other branches of the Government was a luxury that could not be tolerated in time of war. The answer to your question is, therefore, No. There could – or, rather, should – have been no visitors to those rooms.'

'Thank you, sir,' said Mallett. ' I think that covers all we have to ask you.'

'Very good; and now I have something to ask you, Inspector. What is the explanation of this extraordinary incident of your report that lost itself and was found again?'

Mallett concisely recounted the facts of the disappearance and rediscovery of the report, and Mr Palafox listened with grave attention.

'I dislike repeating myself, but after listening to you

I am more than ever concerned at this matter,' he said, when the inspector had finished. 'And have you no hope of identifying the person responsible?'

'I would not go so far as that, sir, but the circumstances make it a very difficult inquiry.'

The Controller sighed.

'It is hideous to contemplate such things occurring in a department under my control,' he said. 'But what can one expect with the material at one's command? The temporary civil servant is the bane of government in war-time.' He looked up, caught a furious glance from Miss Unsworth, and concluded hurriedly, 'With exceptions, of course, with very marked exceptions. But I must detain you no longer. Good day, gentlemen, good day.'

As the two detectives were leaving the room, Mallett turned back to say, 'Would there be any objection, sir, to our having the use of one of the vacant rooms for the purposes of our inquiry? We shall want to interview several members of your staff, and it would be a very great convenience ——'

'Certainly, that shall be arranged. Miss Unsworth, will you please see that these gentlemen are accommodated and that they have everything they require?'

'Well,' grunted Jellaby, as they settled down in Mr Bissett's comfortable room, 'I don't know what we got from that interview.'

'I do,' replied Mallett with a grin. 'We've got a room of our own in the Control, where we can see people without disturbing them or being disturbed. Do you think I could persuade the Unsworth to send for Miss Clarke if I spoke to her very sweetly over this telephone?'

The interview with Miss Clarke was not a particularly easy one, nor did it prove very rewarding to the investigators. They learned from her, what they knew already, that Miss Danville had been an extremely inefficient member of the Licensing Section, and they heard, with unimportant variations, a repetition of the scene in the lounge of the Fernlea Residential Club on the evening before her death. Miss Clarke professed herself to have been seriously shocked by what had occurred on that occasion.

'I had always considered her to be seriously lacking in common sense,' she said. 'Obviously she was not entirely normal. She was so religious, for one thing. I don't mean I have anything against religion, in its proper place, of course, but poor Miss Danville was – well, *morbid* is the only word for it. But I had no idea that she was really *mental*. Naturally, the moment I realized it, I determined to speak to the Establishment Officer about her. It is hardly fair on the rest of the Section to have a person in that condition working with them. If I had had my way she would not have come to the office on Friday at all. She was in no state to work.'

'Why did she insist on coming to the office on Friday?' Mallett asked.

Miss Clarke shrugged her shoulders impatiently.

'She said something ridiculous about wanting to make the office tea. But that was quite absurd, of course. In any case, if that was all she meant to do – and certainly it was all she was fit for – why on earth should she have come in the morning? But it is impossible for anyone to say what was in her mind. You can't judge her behaviour as though she was a normal person.'

'At all events, she did go to make the tea in the ordinary way, with the results that we know. Tell me, Miss Clarke, where were you at that time?'

'In my office, waiting for my tea.'

Jellaby produced a plan from his pocket.

'The Establishment Officer kindly lent me this yesterday,' he explained. 'Let me see, your Section works *here*, does it not?'

'That is right.'

'Only two doors down the corridor from the pantry, I see,' said Mallett. 'And when you speak of your office, you mean this small part partioned off from the rest of the room?'

'Quite.'

'It has no exit of its own to the corridor?'

'No. There was a suggestion of having one made, but I considered that it would promote better discipline among my staff if I were to go through the main room whenever I came in or out. It gives me an opportunity of noticing, unobtrusively, whether work is being properly attended to or not.'

'I follow. Then on Friday you were in your office the whole afternoon?'

'After my return from speaking to the Controller and the Establishment Officer, yes.'

'Can you tell us whether any of the members of your Section were absent during that time?'

'They were all in their places when I returned. After that, I could not tell you. I was particularly busy, and I remained in my own office until, on hearing a disturbance, I came out to find Mrs Hopkinson in a state of great excitement and learned what had occurred.'

Miss Clarke waited while Jellaby jotted down a few notes and then said, 'I will return to my work now, if you will allow me. I happen to be particularly busy this morning.'

'Just a moment, if you don't mind,' said Mallett. 'There are some other questions which I should like to ask you. Firstly, would you say that Miss Danville had any enemies?'

'No,' said Miss Clarke without hesitation. 'You

couldn't feel enmity towards a useless creature like that. She was very annoying and aggravating in her silly way, but that's not the same thing. She certainly had no friends, except for that ridiculous Mr Phillips and Miss Brown whom he was always running after. Even Mr Pettigrew only tolerated her. But enemies – no. If you want to know the truth about this business, she did it herself, just to avenge herself on other people by causing them a lot of trouble.'

Mallett made no comment on this theory. Instead, he asked, 'You don't think that Miss Danville may have made any enemies as a result of her attitude towards what was known as the Plot?'

But at this Miss Clarke shut up like a clam. She had nothing whatever to say about the Plot. At first she endeavoured to convince the detectives that she had never heard of its existence, and even when Mallett had gently manoeuvred her out of this untenable position she remained sullenly uncommunicative. It had nothing whatever to do with the case, she persisted. It was just a silly game got up to pass the time among some of the people in the Control, and if she had taken any part in it it was only in order to see that it did not go too far. She refused to divulge any of its details, of which she professed herself largely ignorant. Jellaby was all for pressing her further, and exposing what he felt convinced was a manifest lie, but Mallett forbore. He quickly formed the opinion that Miss Clarke was by now heartily ashamed that she should have imperilled her official standing by taking part in anything so irresponsible and was simply anxious to forget her participation in the undignified affair as quickly as possible. He moved on to another subject.

'There is one other possibility on which I should like your opinion, Miss Clarke,' said Mallett. 'I am sure I can rely on your discretion to treat it as a matter of confidence. There have been suspicions that confidential matters have been allowed to leak outside the Control with the assistance of individuals within it.'

Miss Clarke was properly shocked at the suggestion.

'I have never heard of such a thing,' she said at once. 'And I am quite certain Miss Danville could have had no part in anything of the kind. She hadn't the sense, to begin with.'

'That may be so. The possibility remains, however, that she might have detected someone else in an irregularity − −'

Miss Clarke laughed outright.

'Irregularity?' she exclaimed. 'My good man, Miss Danville's official career was simply a series of irregularities. How would she know if anyone else was acting irregularly or not? She never succeeded in grasping the simplest principles of the office system.'

'None the less, if she were to have seen somebody − let us say − abstracting papers to which he was not entitled − −'

'She'd have thought it the most natural thing in the world. I'm not exaggerating, Inspector. You have no idea what a scatter-brained creature she was. When I think how she let Mr Edelman walk away with the Blenkinsop file, without a transit slip or anything! It was the merest chance I found out where it had gone to. And when I did get it back it was in the most shocking state. It was disgraceful.'

Nothing in Mallett's face betrayed the smallest interest in the Blenkinsop file.

'Really?' he said drily. 'Well, I see that you cannot help us any further, Miss Clarke. Thank you very much. Would you be good enough to ask Mrs Hopkinson to give us a few moments of her time?'

'It's the Government's time, not hers,' retorted Miss Clarke tartly, as she retired. 'But I'll send her along.'

After she had gone, the two men looked at each other.

'Edelman and Blenkinsop,' said Jellaby. 'Curious.'

'Very,' said Mallett. 'It looks as if this inquiry might help me to clean up the other affair after all. It would be satisfactory to kill two birds with one stone.'

'Side issue,' said Jellaby firmly. 'I'm not interested.'

'I know you're not. But think how happy we should make the Controller! However, we'll leave that at the back of our minds for the present. Just now, let's concentrate on Mrs Hopkinson.'

It was, indeed, quite an effort to concentrate on Mrs Hopkinson. She had been ever since the result of the inquest became known in a state of bottled-up excitement, and the summons to be interviewed by the police had the effect of drawing the cork.

'This is simply the most *ghastly* business!' she exclaimed, before a question could be put to her. 'Honestly, I never dreamt that someone had actually done her in! I was actually there at the time, you know, and I hadn't the ghost of an idea. You could have knocked me down with a feather when I heard. Who could have wanted to hurt the poor old soul? That's what I want to know.'

'So do we all,' said Mallett drily. 'Now, Mrs Hopkinson, suppose you help us by answering a few questions.'

'Rather! Anything you like, of course. But of course, I don't honestly know a thing, except simply that when I found the door was locked – –'

'What were your movements on Friday afternoon?'

Mrs. Hopkinson looked somewhat dashed at the abrupt question.

'Ooh,' she said doubtfully. 'I dunno. The usual, I suppose. I had lunch in the canteen, with Judith Clarke actually. Then I went back to the office and worked away like a good girl till tea-time.'

'You didn't leave your work, then, till you went to the pantry to see what had happened to Miss Danville?'

'No. . . . Wait a sec, though, that's not quite right. I've got to be awfully particular, talking to the police, haven't I? Let's see. I was working when the whistle affair from that kettle started to blow. Miss Danville rushed out straight away. She had the door open and was listening for it. She was a bit deaf, you know, but this time she heard it right away. Then I slipped out after her and went into the you know what.'

'You mean the ladies' lavatory?'

'That's right.'

'The entrance to that is on the opposite side to your room,' said Jellaby, looking at his plan, 'and next door to the pantry?'

'Yes. Well, I was in there quite a bit. Nobody else there, so far as I could see. And then when I came out, blessed if the old whistle wasn't still going hard. So I came along to see what was up. I thought she was saying her prayers in there, or something. She used to do that sort of thing, you know – go off into a holy swoon when you weren't expecting it. Quite uncanny, it was. Well, of course, I found the door locked, and just then Miss Brown came along with Mr Pettigrew.'

'I think we know what happened after that,' said Mallett, to the evident disappointment of Mrs Hopkinson, who felt herself unfairly baulked at the most thrilling point in her recital. 'Now, I'd like to ask you about another point. Had Miss Danville any enemies, so far as you know, among the other workers in the Control?'

'If you mean me,' said Mrs Hopkinson belligerently, 'I'll tell you straight out. I didn't like her, and I don't mind admitting it. I had a jolly old row with her only the night before. But it doesn't mean that every time I have rows with people I go about sticking things into them, I'd have you know.'

'Nobody has suggested that yet, Mrs Hopkinson.'

'I dare say not, but I like to know where I am, and I like other people to know it too. And what's more, I don't mind telling you what the row was about.'

'You need not trouble. It was about her encouraging Mr Phillips's attention to Miss Brown, was it not?'

'Oh,' said Mrs Hopkinson, rather deflated, 'so you know about that, do you?'

'I think the immediate cause of the trouble was that you told Miss Danville that Mr Phillips was a married man?'

'Yes. And a proper fool I made of myself, I don't mind telling you. It's no good asking me where I got the idea from, but I was as positive of it as I am that I'm standing here. And when I get an idea like that in my head I just can't help letting it out. I'm like that. I just couldn't bear to see a young girl being taken in. When Mr Pettigrew told me he could prove Mrs Phillips really was dead, I was struck all of a heap. And he fairly put the wind up me, talking about law actions and things. But it's no good holding that against me now, because I got in first with Mr Phillips that very night, before I went to bed. I just told him straight what I'd said and how I knew it was wrong now and so did Miss Danville, and I must say, he was ever so nice about it – took it ever so quietly, quite like a gentleman. Not that he is one, really,' Mrs Hopkinson added by way of an afterthought, 'and I still maintain that he's only after Miss Brown's money. But I don't see how he could sue me after he'd taken my apology, do you?'

'Suppose we get back to Miss Danville,' said Mallett,

when Mrs Hopkinson's eloquence had at last run down.

'Miss Danville? Well, there's nothing much else to say, is there? She was a proper nuisance, always messing things up in the office, and I just couldn't stand the way she was always egging Miss Brown on to marry Mr Phillips. Not that I ever heard her, you know, but I'm sure she was. What she ever saw in him, I don't know. If Miss Brown wanted to marry an old man, why didn't she take Mr Pettigrew? Anyone could see with half an eye that he would have her if he could. Ooh! That's an idea, isn't it? Suppose Mr Pettigrew killed Miss Danville because she was the one who stood in the way of his marrying Miss Brown? You are asking about enemies, Inspector. He's the one who was her real enemy, or ought to have been.'

Mallett's moustache points were quivering, but he contrived to keep his voice steady as he said, 'You have already nearly got into trouble once, Mrs Hopkinson, from making accusations which proved to be unfounded. You had better be a little more careful in future.'

'Right oh!' said Mrs Hopkinson, unabashed. 'It was just an idea that came into my head all of a sudden, so to speak. I won't breathe a word to anyone, honest I won't. Is there anything else, because I don't mind telling you, it's getting on for my dinner time?'

'Only this. Would you like to tell us anything about what was known as the Plot?'

'Oh, the Plot! The poor, giddy old Plot! You don't imagine that could have anything to do with it, do you? It was just a rag, really. It all started the night we found out Mr Wood wrote detective stories. Then it grew and grew, and he kept suggesting things and Mr Edelman kept suggesting things, till my poor head simply couldn't hold all the stuff they were going to put into it.

I wanted to turn it into a play and have it acted as a Christmas jollification, but the others wouldn't hear of it, and after that I got a bit fed up with it, to tell you the truth. It all seemed a bit silly, really, carrying on like that. Still we did get quite a kick out of it, and it was rather a lark, creeping about the place, working out how Miss Danville was to murder the Controller without anyone knowing.'

'It was rather too much of a kick for Miss Danville, when she found out,' Mallett observed.

'Oh, that was all Mr Rickaby's fault. He never had any call to let it out like that. He's a nasty bit of work, and we oughtn't never to have had him in it at all.'

'But if you had made a play of it, as you wanted, Miss Danville would have found out just the same,' the inspector pointed out.

'Yes, but that'd have been different. More of a rag, I mean. Of course, she was bound to know sometime, I admit. Mr Edelman kept on saying he wanted to see her reactions. Well, he got her reactions good and proper. My word, he did!'

'You spoke of "creeping about the place" just now,' said Mallett. 'That was, in fact, just in the neighbourhood of the pantry, was it not?'

Mrs Hopkinson nodded.

'It sounds awful, doesn't it?' she said. 'But that's the truth. There was me and Mr Edelman and Mr Wood, and I think Mr Rickaby came once, only he played the goat so much we had to warn him off. And then Mr Pettigrew caught us and I didn't half look a fool! That man seems to be always catching me on the wrong foot, so to speak.'

'Did you ever do it again after that occasion?'

'I didn't. What with having to dodge Judith at one end and Mr Pettigrew at the other, I couldn't face it.

I don't know about the others, though. I'd begun to think it a bit silly by then, anyhow.'

'Silly or not,' said Mallett, 'the result of all this was that quite a few people were in a position to know just how and when to get to this particular place without being noticed.'

'That's a fact,' Mrs Hopkinson admitted. 'I just hadn't thought of that before, I give you my word. Ooh, Inspector, d'you think all this Plot business was just a blind to do away with Miss Danville? Because if it was, I hadn't an earthly – I just thought it was a rag, really and truly I did!'

'I'm afraid I can't answer any questions of that sort,' Mallett replied in his chilliest official tone. 'I think that is all I want to ask you, Mrs Hopkinson.'

'Well, I'm for my lunch, and I hope there's something left,' said the lady, and withdrew.

After she had gone, Mallett turned to Jellaby with a deep sigh of relief.

'I don't know about you,' he said, 'but I feel like following her example.'

# CHAPTER FIFTEEN

## Miss Brown and Mr Phillips

'Who do you suggest as our next subject for interview?' said Mallett to Jellaby, when they returned to their temporary headquarters after lunch.

'This Brown person,' answered Jellaby without hesitation. 'She seems to be right in the middle of the whole affair. Come to think of it, she's the cause of all the ructions we've heard about. Everyone in a state about her, one way or the other, before the event. When it happens, she's right on the spot. What the French call a Fem Fatal, if you ask me.'

'That's not exactly the kind of picture of her that I had gathered from Mr Pettigrew,' said Mallett, 'but you may be right, of course. At all events, we'll see what she has to say.'

When Miss Brown arrived, instead of the 'Fem Fatal' of Jellaby's imagination the detectives found themselves confronted by a very unhappy and obviously frightened girl. The first mention of Miss Danville produced a flood of unaffected tears that threatened to put an end to the interview before it had begun. Mallett offered to postpone questioning her until she felt stronger, but she shook her head.

'I shall be all right,' she said at last, screwing her damp handkerchief tightly in her fist. 'I'd rather go through with it now than later. You must forgive me, but Miss Danville was such a very dear person, and so kind to me – I still can't believe this has really happened.'

'You were, in fact, Miss Danville's closest friend at Marsett Bay?' Mallett asked in a tone of sympathy that would have drawn confidences from an oyster. Miss Brown nodded. 'Did she confide in you as to her own affairs?'

'Not very much,' was the reply. 'I don't know that she had a great deal to tell about her life. She had always lived very quietly, you know. I know that when she was quite young – about my age – she had been engaged to be married, but he died suddenly – a motor accident or something – and that had – had upset her very much.'

'Upset her mentally, do you mean?'

'That's a very unfair way to put it,' Miss Brown replied with a good deal more animation than she had shown hitherto. 'Everybody persists in thinking that Miss Danville was mad because she didn't look on things in the same way as other people, when actually all it meant was that her scale of values was different. You see, she believed that the other world was more important than this one, and other people can't understand that. I didn't understand it myself, but I could sympathize with her. It was a belief that meant everything to her – the one thing life had taught her, she used to say.'

'Spiritualism?' Jellaby ejaculated.

'She had at one time been interested in spiritualism, but not for a good many years. I think she had been through many stages in search of truth, but she told me many times that she had found peace at last. I'm sure –' her voice trembled '– I'm sure I hope she has found it now.'

'Did she tell you she had been in a mental hospital?' Mallett continued.

'No. That came as quite a surprise to me when I heard of it. Not that it should have surprised me, I suppose. Sometimes, I know, she did become a little uncertain where this world ended and the other world began, especially if people flurried her or were unkind to her, and I suppose that would have given them an excuse to shut her away. But she never spoke of it.'

'You speak of people being unkind to her. Did she ever say anything that made you think she had an enemy?'

'I am perfectly certain she had none,' Miss Brown declared with emphasis. 'People would get impatient with her in the office because they didn't understand her and see that they ought to make allowances for her, and other people used to laugh at her, as even Mr Pettigrew did until – until I asked him not to. But that wasn't the same thing at all. She was much too good and kind and harmless to have ever made an enemy.'

Mallett leaned back in his chair and glanced at Jellaby, to see whether he had any further question to put at this point. Jellaby seized his opportunity without hesitation.

'Why was she so keen for you to marry Mr Phillips?' he asked bluntly.

Miss Brown received the question with complete calmness. She did, however, acknowledge that it was unexpected by looking her interrogator firmly in the face. Jellaby shifted uncomfortably in his chair under the candid stare of her unexpectedly brilliant blue eyes.

'She thought I ought to be married,' she replied evenly. 'She believed that everyone had their mission in life – their proper part allotted to them to fill – and she thought that mine would be fulfilled in marriage. When Mr Phillips – when he approached me, I had nobody else to turn to to confide in, and I was very glad of her advice. She liked him very much, but she did not, of course, try to influence me in any improper way, and I shouldn't have listened to her if she had. That is all.'

'Other people didn't approve of the idea, so I gather,' Jellaby suggested.

'I wasn't interested in what other people thought about it,' Miss Brown replied with a touch of hauteur.

'Can you think of any other people who would be anxious for any reason to prevent your marriage to Mr Phillips?' the inspector persisted.

'And kill poor Miss Danville as a way of preventing it?' countered Miss Brown swiftly. 'That seems to me very absurd.'

And indeed, put thus baldly, it seemed very absurd indeed.

'Well, Miss Brown,' said Mallett, 'we are very much obliged to you for answering all our questions. It only remains now for you to tell us what you can remember of the events of last Friday.'

There was, apparently, very little that Miss Brown had to tell, and she seemed very reluctant to tell even that little. Her nervousness returned as soon as the actual events of the days of the murder were touched upon, and her story had to be dragged out of her piecemeal.

She had been to London, on leave, to attend to her private affairs. She had returned by the train which reached Marsett Bay in the early afternoon. Shortly after she reached her office she had heard the kettle begin to whistle. Then Mr Pettigrew had sent her to see what had happened, and she had found the door was locked. That was all she knew.

At what time did she reach the office of the Control? She could not say within a quarter of an hour. How long had she been in her room before the whistle began? She had no idea. How long before Mr Pettigrew sent her to the pantry? She shook her head, hazarding only the opinion that it was 'a minute or two'.

'It must have been a bit longer than that,' said Mallett patiently. 'You see, Mr Pettigrew tells us that he sent you to see why the kettle had not been turned off as soon as you came into his room, and by then it had been whistling for quite a long time – five or six minutes at least, he thinks. It looks as if you must have been in your room for that space of time before you went into his.'

Miss Brown dumbly contemplated her feet for a moment or two before she admitted that it did look like that.

'You can't suggest what you were doing in that time? Did you go to the ladies' lavatory, by any chance?'

No, Miss Brown, rather doubtfully, did not think she did.

'Well, then . . . ?'

Miss Brown passed her hand wearily across her brow.

'I think I was writing a letter,' she said at last.

'Well, that explains it, then,' said Mallett encouragingly. The girl was so obviously tired and unhappy that he felt no wish to prolong the interview any further than was absolutely necessary. 'Only one more question, and we shall have finished. During all this time, did you see anybody in the neighbourhood of the pantry until you went there and found the door locked?'

Miss Brown, still looking at her shoes, silently shook her head.

'Then we need not trouble you any further. Good afternoon, Miss Brown, and if later on you remember anything else about Friday afternoon, you will let us know, won't you?'

'Funny the way she shut up when we came to Friday afternoon,' observed Jellaby after she had gone.

'Yes,' said Mallett. 'It was very noticeable after her readiness to talk about her private affairs. There might be several explanations for that, of course.'

'Shock? Nerves? Guilty conscience?'

'Yes. I should be surprised if it was the last, though. She struck me as a very genuine sort of person.'

'Those eyes of hers,' muttered Jellaby. 'Most surprising. Make her face look quite different when you see them. Very determined expression, they've got. She's a lot tougher than you'd think at first sight, if you ask me.'

'Perhaps it was her eyes that bowled over Mr Phillips, and not her private income, as Mrs Hopkinson seems to think.'

'I'd like to see this Romeo of hers,' said Jellaby.

'You shall. We might as well polish him off now. I shouldn't expect anything too romantic, though, or you may be disappointed.'

If there was nothing romantic about Mr Phillips when, shortly afterwards, he made his appearance before the detectives, that was the only fault that could be found with his demeanour. He was calm, grave, courteous, and consistently helpful so far as his memory served. The interview proceeded smoothly, if somewhat wordily.

'You knew the deceased, Miss Danville, well, Mr Phillips?' was Mallett's first question after the usual preliminaries.

'Very well,' Phillips replied promptly. 'I really got to know her as the result of her friendship with Miss Brown. Miss Brown and I, I should explain – –'

'So I understand. Miss Brown has already told us something of the situation between you.'

'I must say, I wish she would tell me a little more about it,' said Phillips ruefully. 'At present, I'm afraid the position is still a little indeterminate. That is, I have not yet persuaded her to name the day, although I have little doubt. But I fear that I am straying from the point. You were asking me about Miss Danville.'

'You were aware, of course, that Miss Danville was – how shall I put it? – somewhat eccentric in some ways?'

'I knew that she was mentally unstable,' Phillips replied precisely.

'That knowledge, Mr Phillips, must have affected your friendship with her to some degree, surely?'

Phillips paused a little before replying, and when he spoke it was plain that he was choosing his words with care.

'It did affect our friendship, Inspector,' he said finally, 'but not in the way which you might have supposed. Indeed, I may say that my recognition of her infirmity was in the nature of a link between us.'

'What exactly do you mean, sir?'

'What I am about to tell you, gentlemen,' Mr Phillips went on in his precise manner, 'is in the nature of a confidence. It is not a thing that I should ordinarily mention to anyone, and indeed I have not even told Miss Brown about it. There is no reason why I should, and, to be perfectly frank with you, I am only giving the information to you because I know that you would find it out for yourselves if the course of your inquiries happened to turn in that direction, and in a matter of this kind I am anxious to avoid even the semblance of withholding – er – information.' He frowned slightly, as though offended by his own failure to find a synonym for 'information,' cleared his throat, and went on: 'I am a widower – a fact –' he permitted himself a slight smile – 'as to which there appears to have been some doubt in certain quarters. Now my late wife was for some time before her decease an inmate of Bloomington Hospital, Hertfordshire.'

Having thus delivered himself, Mr Phillips looked at Mallett as though to see what the effect of his revelation would be. If he was expecting any reaction from the inspector, he was disappointed, for Mallett's expression of polite attention did not change in any way.

'I should perhaps explain,' he went on, 'that Bloomington Hospital is the official name for the establishment, and has been so for many years. In common parlance, however, it is still better known by its earlier title of Chalkwood Asylum.'

'Chalkwood Asylum!' Mallett echoed. 'The place where Miss Danville herself – –'

'Exactly. And this melancholy coincidence, if I may so describe it, did, as you said just now, affect our friendship in a somewhat unusual way. It was naturally rather painful to me at first to be reminded in this manner of a tragedy in my past life – –'

'Just a moment, Mr Phillips. I appreciate what you say, but there is one point that I should like cleared up before you go any further. When did you learn that Miss Danville had been in this asylum?'

'At quite an early period in our acquaintance,' Phillips replied. 'I am most anxious that there should be no misunderstanding on that point, Inspector. Several months at least before her death she confided in me, and when she realized that my late wife had, in fact, been a fellow sufferer there – though she was never certified, I desire to make that quite clear, she was a voluntary patient only – it was – so to speak – a bond. It was not a matter that we spoke about before others, of course, and least of all in the presence of Miss Brown, but there it was. And indeed, I think I may say that the knowledge that my former marriage had been clouded by the incidence of the distressing affliction which she knew so well made her all the more sympathetic towards my hopes for a second and happier union.'

'Quite,' said Mallett, swallowing a yawn. He found Mr Phillips's grandiloquence rather tedious to listen to on a busy afternoon. 'You put it very clearly, sir. Now since you seem to have been in Miss Danville's confidence more than anybody else, you may be in a position to answer this question: Was there anything in her past or present life that could give anyone a motive for murdering her?'

Phillips shook his head.

'That is what I ask myself,' he replied. 'Who could have wished to lay violent hands on such a harmless, innocent person? She had ill-wishers, certainly – you will forgive me, Inspector, if I do not mention any names – they will all be well known to you, no doubt – but that, after all, is a different thing altogether. I confess to you, I am completely baffled in this matter.'

'In other words, No.' Jellaby's murmur was just audible as he wrote down a brief note. Mallett's moustache points twitched, but he kept his voice steady as he said:

'Just one more question, Mr Phillips. Where were you on Friday afternoon?'

'Let me see. You will appreciate, of course, that this is Tuesday, and until the distressing revelations of the inquest in yesterday's evening papers none of us imagined that it would be incumbent on us to account for our movements at what proved to be the material time.'

'I quite understand, Mr Phillips, but do your best.'

'Certainly I will. On Friday afternoon, then, I was at my desk as usual after my return from luncheon in the canteen, which would be at approximately two-fifteen, until – but stay! Friday was of course the day when Miss Brown returned from leave. Of course, I recollect now.'

'What has Miss Brown's return to do with it?' asked Mallett.

'Simply this. That as Miss Brown had apprised me by telegraph of her intention to travel on the early train, I took occasion to go down to see her for a moment or two in her room as soon as she came in. I cannot tell you the exact time, but no doubt she will have mentioned it to you.'

Mallett said nothing, but Jellaby was unable to suppress a slight start of surprise which Phillips was quick to notice.

'She didn't tell you?' he exclaimed. 'How strange – but I think I can understand. The foolish girl had evidently an idea that in revealing my presence in that part of the building she might be in some way incriminating me. I trust you will not hold it against her in any way, Inspector. This sort of suppression of information is very natural in the circumstances, but it can be very easily misunderstood. I do sincerely hope you will overlook it.'

'Suppose,' said Mallett, 'you were to tell us quite shortly exactly what did in fact happen.'

'It is perfectly simple. Miss Brown, as I mentioned just now, had told me that she was returning by the early train that afternoon. The window near which I work happens to overlook the entrance to the office. I was particularly anxious to have a few words with her in private as soon as possible, and accordingly, when I saw her enter the building I made some excuse, slipped downstairs and went to her room. I was only there a few moments and left, if my recollection is correct, just before the now celebrated whistle began to sound from the kettle near by. I recognize,' Mr Phillips concluded deprecatingly, 'that this places me in rather embarrassingly close proximity to the scene of the – the event at a material time, but I feel bound to make a full disclosure of what actually occurred.'

'Did you see or hear anybody else in the neighbourhood of the pantry while this was going on?'

'No. And I may add that I am fairly confident nobody else saw or heard me.'

'Oh?'

'I can move fairly quietly, and I should say quite frankly that I was not desirous of attracting attention to myself. For one thing, people talk, and I had had quite sufficient gossip directed at myself and Miss Brown already. In particular, I did not wish to make my presence known to Mr Pettigrew. I had already had one accidental encounter with him outside the door of Miss Brown's room which proved somewhat awkward to all three of us, and I was anxious not to repeat the experience.'

'I see.' Mallett appeared sunk in reflection for the moment, which gave Jellaby a chance to intervene.

'What I can't understand,' he said, 'is why you bothered to take all this trouble to say a few words to Miss Brown when you were seeing her that very evening at your lodgings. Can't have been as urgent as all that, surely?'

Phillips smiled. 'I agree that it seems rather inconsistent,' he said, 'but there was a good reason for it. As I said just now, I wished to speak to Miss Brown *in private*. It so happened that in the prevailing circumstances conditions at the Fernlea Residential Club were not very conducive to *private* conversation.'

'Just what do you mean?' asked Jellaby impatiently.

'Merely that, apart from all the natural difficulties inherent to a place of that kind, Miss Danville, though the kindest of persons and the very dear friend of us both, did not always realize that her presence might sometimes be superfluous. That was why on this occasion, as had happened previously, I was driven, much against my will, to trespass on Miss Brown's business hours.'

'Thank you, Mr Phillips,' said Mallett. 'Is there anything else you would like to tell us?'

'I think not – except that I would once more ask you

very earnestly not to make things difficult for Miss Brown on account of her ill-judged but, I am sure, well-meant suppression of the fact of our meeting on Friday afternoon. She is, I know, under a great strain as the result of what has occurred, and I am sure you will not judge her hardly.'

'That is a matter for our discretion, sir, but – we are reasonable people, I hope. Good afternoon!'

'Glib,' was Inspector Jellaby's verdict, when the door had closed behind Mr Phillips. 'Much too glib, in my opinion.'

'He certainly had an answer to everything,' said Mallett.

'But he needn't have made a speech when a plain Yes or No would have done. I always hated talkers, but I suppose some are made that way. There's another odd thing about what he told us which I'm sure you noticed.'

'Do you mean the discrepancies between his story and Miss Brown's?'

'That's right. Contradict each other at every point.'

'Let's see,' said Mallett. 'In the first place, there's the matter of his seeing her in her office on Friday afternoon. I dare say his explanation of her not mentioning that is the true one, and at any rate the fact that he volunteered it is in his favour. Then there's the difference between their accounts of what Miss Danville told them about herself.'

'That's what struck me,' said Jellaby. 'Here's the pair of them, each making out to be her best friend, but they might be talking about two different people. Miss Brown won't even admit she's mad, but she tells Phillips that she's been in an asylum. She tells Miss Brown all about a love affair but never seems to have mentioned it to him. And she seems to have given each of them a different reason for marrying the other.'

Mallett laughed. 'I don't see anything unusual in that,' he said. 'It seems to me only natural that Miss Danville should show different sides of herself to her two friends. The only thing that does surprise me is that Phillips should never have hinted to Miss Brown that she had been in a mental hospital. He must be a very discreet man.'

'He's a very deep one,' said Jellaby with conviction. 'I can tell you one thing in which their stories do agree, though, and agree with everyone else's story so far.'

'And that is – –?'

'No alibis. Not a single soul we've seen, not counting the Controller, can produce a respectable alibi for Friday afternoon. It's uncanny – and I've a notion it's going to make things difficult.'

'Well,' said Mallett, 'perhaps we shall pick up a few alibis as we go along. There are several more people to be seen yet. I don't know what you think, but I'm inclined to try Mr Edelman next.'

# CHAPTER SIXTEEN

## Edelman, Wood, and Rickaby

'WELL? What do you want me for?'

Edelman's tone was less belligerent than his words. Rather he gave the impression of a kindly but busy man interrupted in his important work by the inopportune attentions of children. He was quite prepared to give the children some of his attention if necessary, but none the less they were somewhat of a nuisance.

'I am Detective-Inspector Mallett of the Metropolitan Police and this is Detective-Inspector Jellaby of the County Constabulary,' said Mallett evenly. 'We are inquiring into the death, last Friday, of Miss Honoria Danville.'

'Oh, that!' said Edelman, as if it was the last thing in the world he expected to hear. 'I'm sorry, I can't help you about that. I don't know the first thing about it.'

'In that case, we shan't have to trouble you for very long,' Mallett rejoined equably. 'Won't you sit down?'

'Might as well,' muttered Edelman ungraciously, and flung himself into a chair. Then he said, 'There's only one thing I can tell you about Miss Danville, and I expect you know that already – she was off her head.'

'Did you dislike her very much?'

'Dislike her? No. I thought she was rather amusing – unconsciously, of course. I should probably have hated her like poison if I had had the misfortune to work with her, but as it was I could regard her antics with detachment. I could see she was boiling up for something, but I must admit she surprised me at the end. Her death was really completely out of character.'

'Where were you on Friday afternoon, Mr Edelman?'

'Well, really that's rather a hard one to answer. I can say this – I wasn't in my room, or, rather, the cubby-hole which is dignified by the name of a room. I was on the prowl about the building, picking up things that interested me here and there. It's rather a habit of mine in this office. Miss Clarke disapproves of it, by the way.'

'Were you at any time near the pantry, by any chance?'

'Let me see. I think I know the place. It's near Pettigrew's room, isn't it? I was certainly in that part of the building at some time in the afternoon, but I'm afraid I haven't the least idea exactly when. Sorry to be so vague, but it's some days ago now and I never thought I should be called upon to give an account of my wanderings.'

'Did you hear the kettle whistling while you were in that part of the office?'

'I can't recollect that I did. It is possible, of course, but there are so many extraneous noises in this madhouse that I don't know whether I should have noticed it. I have, thank God! the gift of concentration when I am working.'

'And that is absolutely all you can tell us about the business, is it?'

'Absolutely all.'

'There is one other matter I must discuss with you, Mr Edelman, which concerns Miss Danville more than a little and which I think you are in a position to tell us rather more about.'

'I am quite in the dark as to your meaning, Inspector, but I am entirely at your service.'

'It is an affair which was known to those concerned in it as the Plot, I believe.'

'The Plot! Dear me!' Edelman pursed his lips, then smiled and murmured, 'The gods are just, and of our pleasant vices make instruments to plague us.'

'What's that? I didn't quite catch what you said,' interposed Jellaby, his pencil hovering over his open notebook.

Edelman gravely repeated his words. 'For your information, that was a quotation,' he added. 'I apologize for troubling you with it, but Hamlet's remark seemed particularly appropriate at this moment.'

'Well, for your information those words come out of *King Lear*, not *Hamlet*,' retorted Jellaby, shutting his notebook with a snap. 'But if you think they are appropriate I don't suppose it matters much.'

Edelman threw his head back and laughed. '*Touché!*' he exclaimed. 'After that, I can hardly in decency refuse to tell you all I can. But I still do not see what possible connexion that rather childish affair could have with poor Miss Danville.'

'Perhaps it will prove to have no connexion,' said Mallett. 'But until it is proved, I must deal with it. There are some coincidences between the Plot and the actual facts of Miss Danville's death that are too remarkable to be overlooked.'

Edelman's intelligent face looked serious and thoughtful for the first time.

'Coincidences?' he repeated. 'Let me think. If I read the evidence at the inquest aright, it rather looks as though Miss Danville was killed with what in this establishment would be called a bodkin.' He looked inquiringly at Mallett, who nodded. 'I was afraid so. That is really a very unfortunate coincidence indeed, so far as I am concerned, because the use of a bodkin as a weapon was entirely my idea. Wood, who, like most writers, has no powers of observation at all, was full of the most fantastic ideas for a lethal instrument until I pointed out that he had one under his nose all the time. If I have been the means of putting an idea into a genuine murderer's head, I can only say that I am truly sorry. That's the only coincidence I can think of at the moment.'

'I can tell you of one rather more important,' said Mallett. 'My information is that in its later stages the Plot involved something in the nature of rehearsals, and that these rehearsals took place at or near the very spot where the murder was in fact committed. Further, they were rehearsals for an imaginary crime which was to happen at the same time in the afternoon as the real one, and involved calculations of the movements of the staff of the office, including in particular Miss Danville's. Indeed, except for the fact that the actual murder took place at the opposite end of the corridor and involved a different person, it did in fact follow almost exactly the working out of the Plot. What do you say to that?'

'I have two things to say,' replied Edelman promptly. 'The first is that so far as I was aware the rehearsals you speak of were exactly what they purported to be and nothing else. Nothing could have been farther from my mind than that what we were preparing in play should be carried out in earnest, and I never noticed anything in the behaviour of the other people concerned to indicate that any of them had any such sinister intention. My second point is this: Granted all you say, isn't it really quite natural that these coincidences should exist? After all, we were working out, with the greatest degree of realism possible, the means of committing a crime which involved the isolation at the critical time of Miss Danville, whom we had designated for our murderer. Anybody who was planning a real crime, directed against Miss Danville, would naturally plan along the same lines.'

'That is an interesting point ––' Mallett began.

'Besides,' Edelman persisted, 'it isn't even necessary to suppose two minds working independently along the same lines. We didn't exactly make a secret of our plans. Nobody in the Fernlea could help hearing about them. And as Wood was continually making notes of them, which he left about quite freely, anybody working in his department might have come across them. Actually I found one of his drafts slipped inside a file of his only the other day. But I am afraid I interrupted something you were about to say.'

'What I was about to say, Mr Edelman, has only been confirmed by your last remarks. It is that you are evidently a man of more than ordinary intelligence.'

Edelman bowed his head in polite agreement.

'That being so,' the inspector pursued, 'I think it would be only fair if you treated me also as a person of some powers of reason.'

'I hope I do, Inspector.'

'Well, I shall not be satisfied that you are doing so until you have given me some explanation of the part which you have been playing in what seems, on the face of it, to have been a completely crazy, time-wasting game. Quite frankly, your behaviour seems to have been entirely irrational. I can understand a woman like Mrs Hopkinson being prepared to do anything for the sake of what she would call a "lark", though even she seems to have become bored with it before the end. Mr Wood, as a novelist, may have had some professional interest involved. But what on earth were you doing in this silly business? Apart from conducting a rather cruel experiment at the expense of Miss Danville, what were you getting out of it?'

Edelman did not reply for a moment or two. He appeared to be reflecting, and the smile that lighted up his lean face suggested that he found his reflections amusing.

'Yes, I suppose I do owe you an explanation,' he murmured at last. Then he said abruptly, 'Do you know, when you asked me to see you this afternoon I had no idea it had anything to do with Miss Danville?'

'No?'

'No. I thought it meant that you had tumbled to what I was doing in this *galère* – this hocus-pocus of a *Plot*.'

He pronounced the last word with utter contempt.

'It all began, so far as I was concerned, when I got hold of the Blenkinsop file,' he went on. 'And while I am on that subject, Inspector, may I respectfully congratulate you on the work you have since put into that case? Your second report, in particular, I thought, was quite masterly.'

'So it was you who took my report, was it?'

'Yes, I fear that I was the nigger in that particular woodpile. I hope it didn't cause any very serious derangement in your plans. Rumours have reached me that the Controller was much concerned about the matter. In the past, I have not noticed that the delay of a day or so in the passage of a document from one department to another has produced any trouble, or indeed any comment.'

'Am I to understand, Mr Edelman, that you made use of the rehearsals for the Plot as a cover to abstract documents on their way between departments?'

'That is not quite accurate. It would be more true to say that I made use of the knowledge acquired by the rehearsals to lay my hands on official papers when I wanted them in a hurry. But that was a side issue, really. My real object in prancing about the corridors in secret and acting the fool in the way you have so pungently described was, of course, to keep an eye on Wood.'

'I don't quite follow you.'

Edelman looked pained and surprised.

'But is it possible, Inspector,' he said, 'that you are

still not aware that the source of the leakage of information which has troubled you so much is none other than our novelist friend, Wood? But I am forgetting that I had certain advantages in the matter of investigation which were not open to you. I had more or less the run of the office, and above all I had the good fortune to be Wood's confidant in the matter of the Plot.'

'If you knew this,' Mallett objected, 'didn't you consider it your duty to report what you found was going on?'

'No,' said Edelman. 'Quite frankly I did not. I don't propose to put on any airs about it, but I considered my primary duty was towards my firm, to which I am looking forward to returning as soon as this damned war is over. Please don't misunderstand me. I did not abuse my official position to assist my firm at the expense of the State. I have that amount of conscience – and, in any case, I consider that it would in the long run have been bad business. But I saw no reason why I should not employ part of my time in keeping an eye on the activities of our trade rivals, of whom Wood represents our most dangerous. As I said just now, it was the Blenkinsop affair that gave me my first inkling into what was going on and I decided to follow the matter up. I wasn't much concerned with Wood's crimes and misdemeanours, because I was tolerably certain that he wouldn't get away with them for long, but meanwhile I saw the opportunity of getting a really valuable insight into his firm's business methods, and I decided to follow him up.'

'Then that was what was at the back of the Plot?'

'The Plot was a perfectly genuine affair to begin with. It started as a game to while away the long winter evenings. I had had quite enough of contract bridge as she is played at the Fernlea. A game it remained, so far as Miss Clarke and Mrs Hopkinson were concerned, but before very long Wood saw his chance to use it as a blind for his nefarious activities. At the same time, he was, I think, really interested in its possibilities as a basis for a story. You see, he is really two men in one – a dishonest little business man and an inferior, but none the less serious, literary artist. Quite an interesting psychological study in his way. Almost as interesting as Miss Danville, really. The study of her neurotic reactions to the affair was, of course, an added interest to me. It was a great disappointment when it was cut short in this abrupt fashion. But Wood remained my primary object. It was really rather amusing to watch his clumsy efforts to deceive me, without his having any suspicion that he was being double-crossed himself.'

'Was Wood alone in this business, so far as you know?' asked Mallett.

'No. Your report was quite right in suggesting that he had an assistant. It was an enamelled-faced creature in the typing pool, who spends most of her spare time in various bars with young Rickaby. Wood used to pay her – very poorly, I may say – to make extra carbon copies of letters which he thought might interest him. But she was of very minor importance.'

'One last question, Mr Edelman. When you helped yourself to my report – which I assume you did not show to Wood or to anyone else – –'

'Good heavens, no! Your report remains every bit as confidential as though it had gone direct to Pettigrew. You can rely on that.'

'I am glad to hear it. When you took it, you were, obviously, very close to the door of the pantry?'

'Obviously,' Edelman agreed readily. 'And just to make it quite clear, I timed myself to arrive there as soon as possible after the messenger had dumped his papers on the shelf in the corridor. I actually heard his flat feet as he stumped off up the stairs to his tea. That would mean, of course, that he had just lighted the gas-ring. I can't tell you exactly how long it takes for the kettle to boil – Wood has precise notes of that, naturally – but allowing myself a minute and a half to find the document I wanted, I should have got away at least five minutes before the whistle started. During that minute and a half I saw nobody in the corridor.'

'Thank you,' said Mallett.

Edelman rose to go. 'By the way,' he said from the doorway, 'if, as I suppose, you intend to interview Wood, I think you will find that he is the type to crack up pretty easily under examination. I am assuming, of course, that you are still concerned with the black market business. If my reading of his psychology is correct, he is not a murderer. But that is, of course, a question for you. Good day!'

'What do you make of that?' said Jellaby.

Mallett was rubbing his hands with satisfaction.

'If he was speaking the truth about the Plot, and I'm inclined to think he was,' he said, 'it looks as though one side of my investigation was going to be cleared up pretty quickly. This means that I shall save my face at the Yard, and make the Controller happy.'

'And we're not an inch nearer to arresting Miss Danville's murderer,' added Jellaby gloomily. 'All that we've found out, so far as I can see, is that there's yet another suspect without an alibi.'

'No,' Mallett admitted. 'We still haven't found our missing link, or, if we have found it, we haven't recognized it as such, which amounts to the same thing.' He looked at his watch. 'This is about the time when the famous whistle would have started,' he remarked. 'I wonder whether I could work on Miss Unsworth's feelings so far as to raise a cup of tea?'

Ten minutes later he returned, triumphantly bearing a tray.

'On second thoughts I decided I couldn't face Miss Unsworth again,' he said. "I tried the messengers' room instead. It turns out that Peabody has a brother in the Force, so there was no difficulty there. I've asked him to summon Wood to appear before us in five minutes' time. If Edelman's psychology is right, that will just give him time to get cold feet.'

Wood had a very pale face and a determined expression. Without acknowledging the inspector's greeting he plunged into speech the moment he came into the room.

'You will want to know where I was on Friday afternoon,' he began. 'I think it only right to let you know at once that I have a perfect alibi for the whole of the material time.'

Something like a sigh of relief came from Jellaby.

'As I think you are aware, I work in the Enforcement Branch,' he went on, 'I share a table with Mr Phillips. It is near the end of the room farthest from the door, and next to the entrance to Mr Edelman's office. I have a little sketch plan of it here, if it would be of any assistance to you. Between the hours of three and five-fifteen p.m. on Friday I was there without stirring from my seat. I have a number of witnesses to that effect. Not, I should point out, either Mr Phillips or Mr Edelman. Mr Phillips was out of the room between three-fifty and four-ten. Mr Edelman left his office at a little before a quarter past three and did not return to it until close on twenty minutes past four. But a number of other persons working elsewhere in the room can vouch for my presence throughout the time I have mentioned. I may refer you to Mr Clayton, Mr Walton, Mr Parker – –'

'That is very satisfactory, Mr Wood,' murmured Mallett.

'There is another matter on which I desire to make a statement,' Wood went on. 'I am aware that I have unwittingly placed myself in a position that might be misunderstood as the result of having been responsible for planning the plot of a work of fiction in this office. I am prepared to make the fullest possible disclosure.' He pulled from his pocket an untidy bundle of paper. 'Here are all the documentary materials on the subject – all, without exception. I am keeping nothing back. Please peruse them at your leisure. I know that they may be construed as evidence against me, but I insist that on any fair reading of them it must be plain that the crime to which they relate is purely, entirely, *imaginary!*'

His voice rose almost to a scream on the last words.

Mallett stirred the heap of papers on the desk before him with the tip of his forefinger.

'But surely, Mr Wood,' he said gently, 'if you have a well-attested alibi, it isn't really necessary for me to go through all this? There seems to be a lot of reading matter here.'

Exhausted by his eloquence, Wood gasped two or three times before muttering, 'Of course, if you're prepared to take my word for it – –'

'And the word of Mr Clayton, Mr Walton, and Mr Parker,' Mallett reminded him. 'Surely, that should be enough for anyone?'

'Yes,' Wood admitted, 'I suppose it should.'

'As a matter of fact,' Mallett went on, in the manner of a very large cat playing with a very small mouse, 'although my colleague and I are extremely glad that you are able to provide us with such a good account of your activities on last Friday afternoon – my colleague particularly – I am afraid you have rather jumped to conclusions in volunteering your statement.'

He paused and in very leisurely fashion filled and lit

his pipe. Wood's strained expression meanwhile did not relax and his eyes never left the inspector's face.

'As a matter of fact,' said Mallett, blowing out the match and depositing it carefully in Mr Bissett's ashtray, 'I intended to ask you a few questions about your other activities.'

'My – other – activities?'

'Activities which I can indicate most simply by the name Blenkinsop.'

If Edelman had been present at that moment, he would undoubtedly have been gratified to observe the accuracy of his psychological observations. Wood's face seemed to crumple up. The sharply drawn features became blurred as though the spring that had held them rigid had suddenly snapped. His whole body sagged and slumped forward in his chair. The silence was broken by Mallett's voice, cold and impersonal, administering the official caution.

'I'll tell you everything,' came the answer, in a voice that was only just above a whisper.

A quarter of an hour later, Wood departed, leaving behind him a signed statement, which amounted to a detailed confession. It set out the exact circumstances in which confidential information of the working of the control and instructions for evading it had been conveyed outside. It gave dates, facts, and figures, named individuals and firms. Wood's memory was a good one, and under the inspector's firm guidance, every relevant particular had been included. The shabby little story was complete down to the last detail.

'So that's that!' said Mallett, as he re-read the document before putting it away. 'A miserable little job cleared up. Won't the Controller be pleased!'

'What will they do with him, do you think?' asked Jellaby.

'That's a matter for the Ministry, I suppose. They can either prosecute that poor little rat under the Official Secrets Act or go for his employers for breach of the control and use him as a witness. I hardly think he'll try to go back on this,' he added grimly.

'He certainly made things easy for you, once he started,' Jellaby observed.

'Thank goodness for that! After all, we had nothing whatever to go upon except Edelman's assertion, and that was only in the most general terms. If Wood had chosen to stick his toes in, we should have been able to get nowhere. It's lucky for us that the citizen who knows his rights and has the guts to stand on them is a rare type.'

'Well,' said Jellaby, 'this is all very nice for you, but we're still not – –'

'An inch nearer catching Miss Danville's murderer. I know. Don't rub it in. But we've had one stroke of luck today and we may still have another. There is still Master Rickaby to be tackled.'

The interview with Rickaby, however, proved to be a sad anticlimax. The inspector had not been speaking to him for two minutes before he realized that this unattractive young man belonged to precisely the type that he had just complacently characterized as 'rare'. Rickaby obstinately refused to assist the police in any way whatever. He did not know anything about Miss Danville, he said, and he very emphatically did not wish to be mixed up in any police inquiries. When Mallett resignedly asked him if he would sign a statement to that effect, he promptly replied that he would do no such thing except in the presence of a solicitor.

'I wish you would consult a solicitor,' Mallett said. 'I have no doubt at all that he would advise you to make a full statement, in your own interest.'

'Then I shouldn't take his advice,' said Rickaby truculently. 'Why should I? I've got my rights, haven't I? If I choose to say nothing, I suppose I can. It's no use your trying to use third degree methods on me.'

'Nowadays,' said Mallett quietly, 'people of your sort usually call them "Gestapo methods". You should try to be a little more up to date. And, by the way, if you should find yourself under police observation from now on don't write to your M.P. about it. He might want to know why you're not in the army. Run along now, before I forget I'm a policeman and give you a good smacking.'

Jellaby broke the silence that succeeded Rickaby's departure.

'I'll arrange for the police observation straight away,' he said.

'Please do. It will give him a bit of a fright that'll do him good.'

'What's at the back of his behaviour?'

'Sheer cussedness, I shouldn't wonder. I don't believe he has anything to hide, but simply thinks he sees a chance of scoring off authority. Mr Edelman would probably have something interesting to say about his psychology.'

He rose and stretched himself.

'It's been a tiring day,' he said. 'I have a strong feeling that I have been talking to a murderer during the course of it, and that makes it worse. The whole business seems to me just as illogical as it did this morning, and I can't see my way to put it into shape.'

'And now?' said Jellaby.

'Now,' Mallett replied, tapping Wood's confession, 'I am going to make glad the heart of Mr Palafox. That will be one good deed for the day, anyhow. After that—What time did you say the Gamecock opened?'

# CHAPTER SEVENTEEN

## Illumination at Eastbury

'INSPECTOR MALLETT would like to speak to you, Mr Pettigrew,' said Miss Brown.

Since his visit to Jellaby's office on the day of the inquest, Pettigrew had seen nothing of Inspector Mallett. During the past week he had watched the excitement about the case of Miss Danville rise to a fever pitch, and then slowly subside as day succeeded day without any fresh development. It had been an extremely difficult week to live through. Work at the office had been thoroughly demoralized, and only the efforts of a few staunch devotees of routine, such as Miss Clarke, had succeeded in preserving a semblance of order among the staff. Life at the Fernlea had been almost unbearable. Inevitably the inhabitants had begun to look askance at one another as each became aware that suspicion pointed towards their group. Nothing was said in terms, but feelings showed themselves in an unusually elaborate and distant courtesy of utterance, breaking down now and then into angry altercations over trifles. The sudden disappearance of Wood had relieved the tension momentarily, but when it became known that he had merely been suspended on account of misbehaviour and not arrested for murder, the gloom of mutual distrust settled down on the company again. Naturally enough, Pettigrew welcomed the inspector's reappearance as the sign of a relief from intolerable suspense.

When Mallett came into the room, Pettigrew was quite shocked to see how tired he looked. Colour had deserted his cheeks, there were dark patches under his eyes, and even his moustache points drooped a little. It was the face of a man who had been working long hours under great pressure, and it was not the face of a man who had carried his work to a successful conclusion.

'I came to tell you, sir,' said Mallett in level, expressionless tones, 'that Blenkinsop Limited were committed for trial yesterday on all charges.'

'Oh!' said Pettigrew in a disappointed voice.

The inspector caught his eye for a moment but did not comment on what was in both their minds.

'Both prosecution and defence were anxious for the case to be dealt with as soon as possible, so it has gone to Eastbury Assizes, which start today week.'

Pettigrew pricked up his ears. Eastbury was on his own beloved Southern Circuit. At that moment circuit life appeared to him like an Eden from which he had madly shut himself out. If he could only get away from this dreadful place just for a day or two to the sweet sanity of the circuit mess, he felt that life would be tolerable again. But Mallett was still speaking.

'Mr Flack has been nominated to prosecute,' he said. 'He has suggested that, although a plea of guilty is anticipated, it would be desirable for a witness to attend from this office to prove the receipt of the returns submitted by the defendants.' He coughed and added, 'Mr Flack thought that as legal adviser you might be a suitable person.'

Pettigrew caught Mallett's eye again, and this time he detected something very like a wink.

'Would it be right,' he inquired, 'to describe this arrangement as a wangle between the pair of you?'

'Well, sir,' Mallett admitted, 'Mr Flack did indicate that the circuit had missed you a lot lately, and it occurred to me that in the present circumstances you might be glad of a little change.'

'I am very much obliged to you both,' said Pettigrew, 'and I shall certainly be at Eastbury, though Mr Flack knows as well as I do that the evidence could be given by any of the clerks. Is there anything else you want to tell me, Inspector?'

'I don't know whether you want to hear about the Wood affair, sir. We are still clearing up a few doubtful points and I expect to be in a position to submit a report to you in a fortnight or so. But if you would like to discuss it now — —'

'No,' said Pettigrew. 'Emphatically I do not want to hear about it now — or later, for the matter of that, though then I expect I shall have no choice in the matter.'

'In that case,' said Mallett, looking more tired than ever, 'I have nothing else to tell you this morning.'

'I'm sorry,' Pettigrew said, and the genuine sympathy in his voice broke down the inspector's reserve.

'I'm at my wit's end, Mr Pettigrew,' he confessed, 'and that's the fact. This Danville case has got me down as no case in all my experience has done. Mr Jellaby and I have made every inquiry conceivable, we have interviewed about three-quarters of the staff of the Control, many of them two and three times over, there's a mountain of papers at the police-station which I've been through again and again, and it all adds up to just nothing.'

Pettigrew murmured sympathetically. He could see that it was doing the man good to relieve his feelings.

'It's against all reason!' Mallett burst out. 'Here you have a woman killed in broad daylight in a building crammed with men and women, within a few yards of half a dozen people at least, and there's not a rag of evidence against one of them. The only man of known criminal propensities has a complete alibi. So far as the others are concerned, there's nothing whatever to choose between them on the ground of opportunity, but in not one case is there the faintest trace of motive discoverable.'

'Motive is of course the crux of this case,' said Pettigrew, more for the sake of keeping the conversation going than because he thought he was adding anything original to the discussion. His remark had the effect of setting the inspector off again.

'Somebody wanted to kill Miss Danville,' he said. 'And that's not all. Somebody felt that Miss Danville had to be killed, in a hurry, and took a colossal risk to do it. Why? I tell you, Mr Pettigrew, I've got to find out that reason and lay my hands on that somebody. I've got to! The thought of that person being at large fairly frightens me.'

'It is disturbing,' Pettigrew agreed.

Mallett looked at him strangely.

'Do you realize, Mr Pettigrew,' he said, 'that your own life may be in danger?'

Pettigrew could not help smiling.

'I don't think anybody would go out of his way to eliminate me,' he said.

'I shouldn't be so sure of that,' Mallett retorted. 'Miss Danville would have said the same a fortnight ago. Where you have a hidden motive, who can tell whether he stands in the way of the killer?'

'It's good of you to interest yourself in my welfare,' said Pettigrew. 'But after all there's no reason why I should be picked on especially.'

Mallett's momentary animation had disappeared. He rose from his chair and towered above Pettigrew's desk, a weary giant of a man. Looking into the other's eyes, he said slowly, 'Perhaps there is, Mr Pettigrew.'

A moment later he had gone.

Some time later, Miss Brown came into the room with some letters for signature. Pettigrew read them through and signed them without comment. It occurred to him as he did so that even relations between himself and his secretary had deteriorated during the past week. They seemed now to have nothing to say to each other except what was strictly necessitated by office business. Perhaps it was as well, he reflected. It was always a mistake to mix up human relationships with one's work. There had been a time when he had been quite exercised over Miss Brown's little problems. And now, he felt, he really didn't care a damn. It was a relief to have that worry off his shoulders now. Or was it? He looked up to find her still hesitating beside his desk.

'What is it, Miss Brown?' he asked rather sharply.

'Did – did the inspector have anything to say about Miss Danville?' she faltered.

'No.' said Pettigrew. 'That is – No. He came to talk about the Blenkinsop case,' he added lamely.

Miss Brown, who had, he now observed, been looking very pale of late, went a shade whiter.

'I see,' she murmured.

'That reminds me,' Pettigrew went on, 'I shall be going to Eastbury Assizes next week. I shall be away two nights – or three, if I can spin it out so far. You still have some leave owing to you. Would you care to take it then?'

Miss Brown shook her head.

'Thank you, Mr Pettigrew, but I don't think I shall. As a matter of fact, I had been meaning to mention it – I was thinking of adding my extra days to my Christmas leave.'

'Oh, yes?'

'Yes. And after that' – she hesitated for a moment or two, and then the words came with a rush – 'I don't quite know what my plans will be, but I think I may be leaving the Control altogether.'

So that was that! A week ago she would have said outright, 'I am going to marry Mr Phillips at Christmas.' Well, if she chose to keep her own affairs to herself, thought Pettigrew peevishly, she was at perfect liberty to do so. After all, he had never invited her confidence at any time. All the same, he should have thought – –

What he should have thought, he did not stop to determine. Instead he said drily, 'I see. Well, I shall miss you, Miss Brown.'

Miss Brown opened her mouth as though to answer, but apparently thought better of it, for after standing irresolutely for a moment, she turned abruptly on her heel and walked rather hastily out of the room.

The question of her Christmas leave and what was to follow it was not raised between them again.

The Bar mess at the Blue Boar at Eastbury would have appeared to a stranger a rather ordinary sitting-room in a second-rate country hotel, filled with commonplace men, mostly elderly, talking not very interesting shop. To Pettigrew, in his then mood, it was sheer heaven. He sat back luxuriously in his chair, listening to the ebb and flow of circuit gossip around him. Even the conversation of men whom he had been wont to consider bores now sounded in his ears like exquisite wit.

'Are you prosecuting me for abortion tomorrow, Johnny?'

'I am, my boy. I suppose you're pleading guilty.'

'Pleading guilty! I thought you were going to tell me you were offering no evidence. My client is the most injured, respectable – –'

'– – He was a tartar! When somebody was bold

enough to suggest that the sentence was a bit stiff, he just looked at him and said, "The indictment was wrongly drawn, or I could have flogged the man!" '

Pettigrew smiled. He had invented that story twenty years before, and it was pleasant to find it still going the rounds in not too distorted a form. A hand fell on his shoulder and he looked up to see the Clerk of Assize, beaming with pleasure at the lost sheep returned to the fold.

'Glad to see you, Pettigrew. Are you defending the bigamy tomorrow?'

'Alas! I am neither prosecuting nor defending. In fact, I am here on false pretences. For the time being, I am the lowest thing in the scale of human creation.'

The Clerk's bushy eyebrows met in a frown. 'You're not going to tell me you've been summoned on a jury?' he said incredulously.

'No. I had forgotten jurymen. Besides, they really rank with the animal creation, to judge by the way they are treated. I am that harmless, necessary thing, a witness. I doubt whether I shall even be necessary, as I hardly expect to be called, but in any case tomorrow I shall have the indignity of disputing with you the proper amount of my expenses.'

'I shall make a point of disallowing them,' said the other firmly. 'Meanwhile, what are you drinking?'

After dinner, Pettigrew found that he was not to escape without paying for his holiday. Flack, the most methodical of men, had decided to call a conference with Mallett, and this Pettigrew could not do less than attend. It was a dull enough affair. He listened to Flack expounding a number of Defence Regulations and Orders made thereunder, which he already knew by heart, while Mallett, hardly referring to the mass of papers he had brought with him, dealt competently with the questions of fact. But in the middle of the conference a small event occurred that was to have important consequences.

Mallett was called away to answer the telephone and in his absence Flack raised a point of detail which Pettigrew was quite unable to answer. In an endeavour to be helpful he dived into the inspector's papers in the vain hope of finding the right place in the right file. Opening one of these more or less at random, he was astonished to find his own name in neat capital letters at the head of the page.

'PETTIGREW, Francis': he read: 'barrister; bachelor; no criminal record.' What on earth? He turned back to the beginning of the file, and found that it was headed: 'Danville case Index of personnel.'

'Dear me!' Pettigrew murmured half aloud. 'This is quite embarrassing!'

'What did you say, my dear fellow?' asked Flack. 'Have you got the letter of the 5th April there? I'm sure my copy is incorrect.'

'Sorry,' said Pettigrew, 'I can't find it. We'll have to wait till the inspector comes back.'

He could not resist reading further:

'Born, 1888; called to bar, 1912. Legal adviser to Pin Control since 1st October. Relations with deceased – apparently friendly. Relations with other suspects – mainly negative, but obvious affection for BROWN, Eleanor (q.v.) Query, jealousy of PHILLIPS, Thomas (q.v.)?'

Really, this was too much! Pettigrew could not trust himself to read any further, although the entry under his name covered the rest of the closely written sheet. In disgust, he turned the page over to shut the offending passage from his sight, and found himself confronted with:

'PHILLIPS, Thomas: solicitor's clerk; widower; no criminal record. Born, 1890; married, 1916, Sarah Emily Richards, who died 1934. Employed Messrs. Mayhew and Tillotson, 1919 to 1939. Temporary assistant, Pin Control, since December, 1939.'

Pettigrew had read thus far when Mallett's noiseless reappearance at the door made him hurriedly and rather guiltily close the file and thrust it away beneath the other papers. Thereafter the conference proceeded fairly rapidly to its conclusion. Mallett, who was staying at another hotel in the town, left immediately. If he had noticed Pettigrew's interest in the file of the Danville case, he made no allusion to it. Shortly afterwards Pettigrew went to bed, but it was some time before he could sleep. He was in a mood of intense annoyance – annoyance with himself for having fallen into the temptation of reading what was obviously not intended for his eyes, and double annoyance with Mallett for what he felt to be both an unpardonable piece of impertinence and a most uncharacteristic piece of stupidity. But when this feeling had begun to subside, he realized that there was something else he had read in the file that had struck him. It was all the more irritating in that he could not for the life of him remember what it was. He tossed and turned in his bed for what seemed an eternity, his tired mind nagging at the tiny problem and refusing to be quieted. When at last he found what he was seeking, it proved to be a fact so trivial that his trouble in tracing it seemed utterly disproportionate to the result. Feeling more dissatisfied than ever, but with his mind composed, he finally went to sleep.

Pettigrew was early in court next day, in time to witness the familiar ceremonial of the opening of the Assize. He felt oddly naked, sitting unrobed in the tiny, box-like courthouse where he had so often appeared in the past, and deliberately chose to perch himself upon one of the comfortless public benches at the back rather than join his fellow practitioners further forward. While the commission was being read, he found his mind dwelling, not on the spectacle before him nor on the business that had brought him to Eastbury, but upon his experience of the previous evening. The more he reflected on it – and he could not help reflecting on it – the more irritated he became. A man who always endeavoured to be honest with himself, he forced himself to analyse his feelings, and he quickly came to the conclusion that the real sting in a phrase which might otherwise have only caused him amusement lay in the fact that it came from Mallett, a man whose judgement and penetration he had every reason to respect. Was his complaint, then, thought Pettigrew, relentlessly pursuing the matter while with the outward eye he watched the judge precariously balancing a three-cornered hat on a full-bottomed wig, was his real complaint precisely that there *was* some truth in the remark? Because if so ––

Damn it, no! The inspector was simply being grossly obtuse, and he, Pettigrew, was a fool to imagine that because he had once known Mallett to make a lucky shot in a tricky case he was anything more than a very ordinary, blundering policeman. Remembering now the other matter that had cost him an hour of sleep the previous night, Pettigrew felt all his absurd admiration for him dwindle away. Judgement and penetration indeed! Why, the fellow couldn't even get his facts right! It was too bad! The least one could expect from a man in that position was accuracy in plain matters of details. And a glance – the merest glance – at his own notes was sufficient to convict him of gross carelessness. This from a high officer of Scotland Yard! He felt like writing a letter to *The Times* about it.

There was an additional reason now for Pettigrew's feeling of annoyance, which had long since been transferred from himself to the peccant inspector. He had, as he now recognized, been profoundly shocked and distressed by Miss Danville's murder. He had realized from the start that the inquiry would be a difficult one; but he had taken it for granted that sooner or later it would be resolved. Now he was not so sure. His faith in Mallett had sustained a serious blow. What chances were there of a problem like this being solved by an officer capable of making such egregious – Pettigrew found himself positively mouthing the word – egregious blunders?

At this point in his reflections his train of thought was broken by the movement in court as the judge, the commission opened, left the bench. When he sat down he was for the first time aware that the man who was and had for some time been standing beside him was Mallett himself.

The inspector's trick of silently materializing, often where least expected, was, though professionally useful, apt to be disquieting. To Pettigrew in his then mood it seemed the crowning insult, and his reply to Mallett's genial 'Good morning!' was decidedly taciturn.

'I hope you slept well, sir,' the man went on, as though determined to be tactless.

'As a matter of fact,' said Pettigrew shortly, 'I didn't.'

'I'm sorry about that, sir,' Mallett answered, with his usual look of grave concern. 'I can't say that I got too much sleep myself last night.'

'Oh?' Pettigrew did not feel interested in anybody else's insomnia at the moment.

'No. And it wasn't this Blenkinsop business that kept me out of bed, either. I had a rare lot of stuff in the Danville inquiry to go through again.'

Pettigrew said nothing. Mallett could go through papers till the cows came home for all the good it would do, he was thinking.

'Inspector Jellaby has been putting a lot of work into the case,' Mallett continued. 'A tremendous lot of work. I dare say you noticed, sir, among my papers last night, a very useful little file he has prepared on the personnel of the case.'

'Silence!' roared an usher, and Pettigrew, his mind in a whirl, rose to his feet with the rest as the judge returned to the bench to begin the business of the day. Dimly he felt that he had been making a fool of himself, if only to himself.

'Jellaby did that?' he murmured as they resettled themselves on their comfortless seats. 'Well, all I can say is, from the little I saw of it, it's utterly unreliable.'

Mallett shot a look of pained inquiry at him, but his words died on his lips as the Clerk of Assize called out the names of the first prisoners.

Three weedy young men appeared in the dock and severally pleaded guilty to office-breaking and larceny. Their case disposed of, Mallett turned to Pettigrew again.

'I can't agree with you, sir,' he said. 'Mr Jellaby may not be very subtle, but I can assure you his work is very sound when it comes to facts.'

'I can assure you it's not,' Pettigrew retorted, deliberately ignoring the obvious implications in the reference to Jellaby's lack of subtlety. 'I'll give you one example. I just happened to glance at the page relating to Phillips last night, and I saw that he had put down that Mrs Phillips died in 1934. It's a very small point, but – –'

'There must be silence in court,' came a chill voice of reproof from the bench, and Pettigrew realized that he, the most punctilious of men, had interrupted the reading of an arraignment for bigamy.

'But she did die in 1934,' whispered the inspector, ten minutes later, the bigamist having been dealt with. 'I gave Jellaby the date myself.'

'Then you gave it wrong. She died in 1931.'

'1934.'

'1931.'

'I assure you, sir, I've seen her death certificate and it is dated the 12th of April 1934.'

'But that is nonsense, Inspector. Why, I know for a fact that her will was proved in 1931. The solicitor couldn't have made a mistake about that. I'll show you his letter if you – Oh, Lord! he's calling our case on now.'

The case of Rex v. Blenkinsop, although a plea of guilty, lasted over three-quarters of an hour. It might well have been longer. Flack, for the prosecution, had first to persuade a slightly incredulous judge that such a thing as the Pin Control existed and then to take him through all the relevant Regulations and Orders – a process which his rather dreary manner did not make any the more enlivening – before dealing with the fairly simple facts of the case. The defence had briefed Babbington, the most fashionable and expensive silk on the circuit, and although what he had to say in mitigation could have been put into a couple of sentences he contrived to spin out his address to twenty minutes. Babbington always prided himself on giving his clients their money's worth, and in this case his long-windedness reduced his rate of pay to the very reasonable figure of fifteen guineas a minute. The costs of the defence and the substantial fine which was imposed upon the defendants taken together had the effect of reducing their liability to Excess Profits Tax by quite an appreciable amount.

While all this was going on, the officer in charge of
the case and the official witness for the prosecution sat
side by side, their thoughts miles away from the matter
in which they were nominally engaged. Had either of
them been called upon to give evidence, he would have
made a very indifferent figure in the witness-box. Pettigrew was puzzling over a problem which seemed at first
sight completely unimportant and which left to himself
he would probably have dismissed as an unaccountable
aberration on the part of a normally reliable solicitor.
But he was aware that Mallett, ordinarily so solid and
immobile, was actually quivering with suppressed excitement. The emotion was contagious, though he could
not guess its cause. Something was in the air, something
more important to him than all the Controls put together. He found himself beginning to quiver too. What
had Mallett got up his sleeve? Would this stupid case
never come to an end?

No prisoner ever waited more anxiously for sentence
to be pronounced than did Mallett and Pettigrew on
this occasion; but when at length the judge finished
speaking neither of them had the vaguest idea what his
decision had been. The last words were scarcely out
of his mouth when the inspector caught his companion
by the arm in a grip that almost made him shout with
pain.

'You mentioned a letter just now, Mr Pettigrew,' he
whispered hoarsely. 'Was that the one you showed Miss
Danville the night before she was murdered?'

'Yes.'

'Giving the date of Mrs Phillips's death as 1931?'

'Yes.'

'And you told Mrs Hopkinson about it too?'

'Yes, but what – –'

'The link, sir! I don't know what it means yet, but I

believe I've found it at last! The link I've been hunting all this time!'

Pain seemed to have made Pettigrew suddenly clairvoyant.

'By God, Inspector, I believe I see it!' he exclaimed. 'If the thing could be done that way, that's how it was done! But could it? That's what we've got to settle!'

Completely oblivious now to the niceties of behaviour in court, he stumbled noisily out, dragging the inspector after him. In the corridor they saw Flack coming towards them, his owl-like face bearing a self-satisfied expression.

'Well, Pettigrew,' he began on catching sight of him, 'I don't think that was a bad result, do you? A bit tricky, these Regulations, but I don't think I dropped any bricks.'

'Bricks? My dear chap, I didn't hear so much as a pin drop.'

'D'you know, I thought at one moment the judge was going off the rails about Paragraph 2AC, but I think I managed – –'

'Look here,' said Pettigrew, interrupting him without ceremony, 'were you or were you not a solicitor before you were called to the bar?'

'Was I a – –? Why bring that up at this time of day? Certainly I was a solicitor, for several years in fact.'

'An active, working attorney, proving people's wills and all that sort of thing?'

'A very active attorney, I assure you.'

'You do know how to prove a will? You have actually done it?'

'Of course, I have. Dozens of them, I should say. But what's all this about, Pettigrew? You look quite warm!'

Pettigrew steered him into the robing-room without replying.

'I hope you're not asking me to become your executor,' Flack went on, removing his wig. 'Because I really think – –'

'I'm not asking you to become my executor. I'm not asking you to think. I'm not asking you to do anything the least difficult. All that the inspector and I are asking you to do is to solve a perfectly simple little case of murder that's been worrying our heads off the last two weeks.'

## CHAPTER EIGHTEEN

### *Explanation at Marsett Bay*

'ONE is,' said Pettigrew – apologetically – 'so appallingly ignorant.'

Inspector Jellaby murmured his polite disagreement.

'Appallingly ignorant,' Pettigrew repeated. 'After thirty years at the bar, I thought I knew as much about my trade as the next man. In fact, I think so still. But I never realized till now what a highly specialized trade it was. It makes me feel like the kind of motor driver who takes the machinery of his car for granted and is astonished at things that are commonplaces to any garage hand. I may know a bit of law, but here's a whole tract of the machinery of the law that is simply a closed book to me.'

'Look here, sir,' said Jellaby rather gruffly, 'it's all very well for you to talk about closed books and such, but this whole case is still a closed book to me. I got Mr Mallett's wire this morning. I arrested Phillips within an hour. I've got a statement from him which I can't make head or tail of except that it amounts to a confession of murder. I am still in the dark. Why did Phillips kill Miss Danville?'

'He killed her,' said Mallett, 'because she was in Chalkwood Asylum at the same time as the late Mrs Phillips.'

'But we knew she was,' Jellaby protested. 'We've known that a long time. Why should that be a motive for murder?'

'Well, the trouble was,' said Pettigrew, 'that Mrs

Phillips wasn't supposed to be there at the time. In fact, she wasn't supposed to be anywhere at all.'

Jellaby looked despairingly from one man to the other. 'Will one of you gentlemen please tell me what it is all about?' he exclaimed.

Pettigrew looked at Mallett inquiringly.

'I think it had better be you, sir,' said the latter. 'For all your talk of ignorance, I think you've got the hang of it better than I have.'

'Very well. I shall deliver my lecture with all the confidence of a student who has just been primed by a good crammer – in this case, Mr Flack, who is a chauffeur like myself, but had the advantage of serving an apprenticeship as a mechanic. Let me take the legal side first and then see how it applies to the facts of this case. To begin with – have you any idea what happens when you die?'

Inspector Jellaby's jaw dropped and his honest face went rather pink at the unexpected question.

'I beg your pardon. I should have explained that I was dealing exclusively with mundane matters. I am also going on the assumption that you have an estate, large or small, to leave and somebody or bodies to leave it to.'

'Oh, if that's what you mean, sir,' said Jellaby, 'I've made my will, and left everything to the wife. Mr Cartwright, the solicitor here, has got all the papers, and I take it that when my time comes he'll do the needful.'

'Exactly. I am in the same position, except that there is no wife in my case. And neither you nor I have any but the most rudimentary idea what the needful is. Your solicitor gives you – or rather your widow – papers to sign and forms to fill up and in due course he hands over the assets of which the estate consists, less the cut taken by the State in the form of death duties, his own costs and expenses, and any legacies you may have made to the local dogs' home, pigeon fanciers' benevolent association or what have you. Precisely how it's done is his affair. You rely on him to do the job and for anybody bred in a solicitor's office it is a perfectly straightforward, rule-of-thumb affair. At this point I may perhaps remind you that Phillips was bred in a solicitor's office.'

'I hoped we should be coming to him soon, sir,' said Jellaby.

'I'm sorry to disappoint you, but we still haven't settled the point, what the needful is. I'll put it as shortly as possible, and leave out all the innumerable complications which can occur, but none of which are present in this case. Mr Flack, I may say, left out nothing. He's not that kind of man. I'll take the simple proposition of a wife making a will and leaving everything to her husband, who is also sole executor; the estate consisting of stocks and shares and the usual little bits and pieces most people have about the place. What does the husband have to do to lay his hands on the cash? It's quite simple really. First of all he has to satisfy the vultures of the Inland Revenue, so he makes out an account of the whole of the goods and chattels of the deceased, giving the proper value to every item. This he summarizes on a form known officially as A – 7, but to solicitors by the more intimate, or kennel, name of Inland Revenue Affidavit. I have one of these charmers here,' Pettigrew went on, producing an eight-page form printed on stout blue paper. 'I lifted it off one of my ex-clients at Eastbury, much to his surprise. It is a solemn thought, by the way, that there is one of these in waiting for each of us. Golden lads and girls all must form the subject of an Inland Revenue Affidavit sooner or later – and the more golden they are, the more intricate the affidavit will be. Most of it, you will see, is made up of forms of accounts – wide open spaces in which wealth of every sort and kind can be analysed for the benefit of the tax-gatherer. There'll be a lot of blank spaces when mine comes to be made out. The affidavit itself covers only two pages, and has a mere seventeen paragraphs. I am now going to read you the relevant parts of it. Be brave. It won't take long, and, to add a little human interest, I shall insert real names and particulars:

'In the Estate of Sarah Emily Phillips deceased.

'I, Thomas Phillips, of such-and-such an address, make oath and say as follows:

'1. I desire to obtain a grant of probate of the will of the above-named Sarah Emily Phillips deceased who died on the 19th day of September one thousand nine hundred and thirty-one aged - -'

'But she didn't,' Jellaby objected.

'Students are requested not to interrupt the lecturer. I was just coming to a nice bit about being domiciled in that part of Great Britain known as England. But let it pass. That is as far as I need go with this elegant composition, anyway. What happens next? When he has settled with the Inland Revenue, our bereaved gentleman sends the deceased's original will to the Probate Registry. Along with it he sends the account, duly receipted by the Inland Revenue, and' – Pettigrew produced another, smaller, printed form – 'the Executor's Oath. Here it is. Only five paragraphs this time, and I shall spare you four of them:

'In the Estate of Sarah Emily Phillips deceased.

'I, Thomas Phillips, et cetera, make oath and say as follows:

'1. That I believe the paper writing hereto annexed and marked by me "T. P. 1." to contain the true and original will of Sarah Emily Phillips of such-and-such address deceased who died on the 19th day of September 1931, at Bloomington Hospital, Herts.'

'But she didn't!' Jellaby repeated. 'She died on the

12th of April, 1934.' He looked at Mallett for confirmation.

Mallett grinned back at him.

'I think you'd better let Mr Pettigrew tell this in his own way,' he said.

'I am obliged to you, Inspector, for trying to keep order in the class. None the less, to gratify the unseemly impatience of my audience, I am prepared to disclose that he is perfectly right. Mrs Phillips died, as her death certificate states, on the 12th day of April 1934. But — and this is the whole point of the case — the documents relating to her estate, which are at this moment lodged in the principal Probate-Registry for that part of Great Britain known as England, are precisely in the form which I have been reading to you.'

'You don't mean to tell me, sir, that Phillips proved his wife's will while she was still alive?'

'That is exactly what I do mean. Strictly speaking, we haven't got to Probate yet, but I can finish the saga very shortly. On getting the papers I have mentioned, all apparently in apple-pie order, fortified by oaths and affirmations and the blessing of the Inland Revenue, with the name of a respectable firm of solicitors to the estate, the Registry grants probate of the will. And why not? I'm sure I should in their place. They are busy people and can't spare the time to go nosing round asylums to see if some poor body is still lingering there when she's supposed to be under the ground. They hang on to the will but send the executor a neat little photographic copy and a document called in the best circles the Probate Act. Once he has this in his hands, all is serene for our friend. It is all he needs to collect the goods of which the estate consists. By virtue of it, stocks and shares in companies are transferred from the deceased's name to his, cash at the bank in her account is switched into his account, and so forth. But there is one rather interesting exception to the rule. It is one that proved quite expensive to Phillips, incidentally.'

'What may that be?'

'The exception is – or are – Life insurance companies. I suppose their trade makes them particularly suspicious and cynical, but the fact remains that before they will cough up, they require to see not only the probate of the will, but also the death certificate. And that, of course, was the one bit of paper Phillips couldn't produce. So when he set to work to get in his wife's modest estate, he had to forgo the very useful little sum of five hundred pounds for which she was insured. That explains a small matter that has been puzzling me ever since I made some amateurish investigations of my own into the *affaire* Phillips. Without going quite so far as Mrs Hopkinson – by the way, I think we all owe her a handsome apology – I did feel a bit dubious about Phillips, and when the lady whom he proposed making his second wife started asking me questions about life insurance I became thoroughly alarmed. I made inquiries, and back came the answer. Mrs Phillips had been insured all right, but the policy had been allowed to lapse for non-payment of the premiums. That satisfied me at the time, but thinking it over afterwards I was rather mystified. For a man so insurance minded as he obviously was, it seemed a bit out of character. Now we know the reason. Nobody is going to go on paying premiums on a policy which he can never collect.'

Inspector Jellaby blew out his cheeks in a prolonged sigh.

'Well, I've certainly learned something,' he said. 'Now let's see how this all works out.'

'It works like clockwork,' said Mallett. 'This is how it goes. Phillips is married to a lady with a bit of money of her own – not much, but perhaps a hundred or a hundred and fifty a year. She makes a will in his favour. Later, she goes off her head and is sent to Chalkwood.'

'As a voluntary patient,' put in Pettigrew. 'She wasn't certified, or the Board of Control would have got hold of her affairs and this jiggery-pokery could never have happened.'

'Quite so. She goes to Chalkwood, a private institution, supported by charity, where the fees are kept low for those who can't afford much.' He turned to Pettigrew. 'What exactly happens to her money while she is there, sir?' he asked.

'I can answer that one. There's a department at the Law Courts which looks after these things. Phillips would apply there and get himself made receiver of his wife's income. Otherwise he couldn't get at it at all. He would have to send in an audited account every year to prove that he was using it for her upkeep – which must have been galling to a man of his type – and of course he couldn't touch the capital while she was alive.'

'While she was alive. Quite so. Well, in September 1931, like a good many other people just then, Phillips finds himself hard pressed for cash. He finds that he could make very good use of his wife's capital, so he carries out this scheme of making believe that she is dead.'

'Would the department you mention be satisfied with the production of the Probate Act, Mr Pettigrew?'

'Surely. The Probate Registry is all part and parcel of the Royal Courts of Justice too. Dog doesn't doubt dog. I dare say he would have to swear another affidavit to get the receivership discharged, but what's an odd affidavit or two to our Mr Phillips?'

'Very good,' Mallett went on. 'Then two and a half years later she does die in fact and there is, apparently, an end of the matter. All that has happened is that he has come into her fortune that much earlier than he should have done. It was just his bad luck that one of the inmates at the hospital at the time of her supposed death happened to be Miss Danville.

'Years later, Phillips meets at Marsett Bay another young woman with a bit of money of her own, and he thinks that here's a good opportunity for a second marriage. Everything seems to go swimmingly, but it so happens that one of the young woman's closest friends here is that same Miss Danville. Miss Danville's memory is none of the best, unless there's something to jog it, and it is quite plain that she never connects him with the Sarah Phillips she knew at Chalkwood, if indeed she remembers her existence at all. Phillips, of course, has no idea that she was ever inside the place.'

'But that wasn't what he told us,' said Jellaby.

'To be sure it wasn't. And it was the fact that he told us such an obvious lie that made me ready to suspect him. If Miss Danville had told him that she had been in the asylum with his wife, who had certainly died there, why should she have believed Mrs Hopkinson's slander for a moment? Phillips slipped up badly there, but I didn't grasp the point of it till much later. That brings me to the evening before Miss Danville's murder. You will remember what happened. As the result of Mrs Hopkinson's suggestion that Phillips was a married man, Miss Danville became so distraught that Mr Pettigrew thought it necessary to prove to her in black and white that Mrs Phillips was dead. He showed her a letter which stated that Mrs Sarah Emily Phillips had died in September 1931. The effect on her was very violent and rather surprising.'

'It certainly was,' said Pettigrew.

'I think we can easily guess what was passing through

her mind at that moment. For the first time, she realized that the late Mrs Phillips was her acquaintance, Sarah Phillips, and she saw to her amazement that she was supposed to have died at a time when she knew her to have been alive. Of course, she didn't know all that we know now, but she knew enough to make it quite plain that something was very seriously wrong and that she had been doing a terrible thing in encouraging Miss Brown to marry this man. Obviously, her first impulse would be to tell her about it at the earliest possible moment.'

'Miss Brown wasn't there to be told,' said Pettigrew. 'And so her first impulse was to tell me, and alas! I wouldn't listen.'

'That is so. Now, what about Phillips? He was, of course, out of the room when Mr Pettigrew showed Miss Danville the letter. He came in just in time to hear her outburst when Rickaby's drunken stupidity, on top of the shock she had already received, produced her breakdown. He then learned for the first time that she had been in the same asylum as his wife, and at the same period. That must have been a serious blow to him. But not a fatal blow. That was to come later on that evening, when Mrs Hopkinson approached him to apologize for having slandered him. Do you remember her words to us about that? "I told him straight what I'd said and how I know it was wrong now *and so did Miss Danville.*" How did she know? I can hear Phillips ask. And the answer was, because Mr Pettigrew had shown her a letter from the late Mrs Phillips's solicitor, confirming the fact of her death. One can imagine Phillips's thoughts when he went to bed that night. He knew, of course, that the letter would contain the date of death which he had given on the Inland Revenue affidavit. He knew that Miss Danville was the one person who was aware that it was a false date. As a matter of course she would tell Miss Brown what she had discovered. Unless he could eliminate her before she could speak to Miss Brown, there was an end of his chance of a comfortable marriage and in its place a fairly certain prospect of a long term of imprisonment for perjury.

'Luck was with him. Miss Danville was too ill to speak to anybody next morning, but she came to the office as usual later in the day. She tried to say something to Mr Pettigrew, but he, very naturally, put her off. Phillips knew when Miss Brown might be expected, as she had telegraphed the time of her arrival. Thanks to Wood and the other plotters, he knew to a minute when Miss Danville might be found alone in the pantry and the chances of finding that part of the building deserted. From his office window he watched for Miss Brown's arrival. Then he slipped along to her room and held her in conversation for a few moments. This had the double object of assuring himself that she had had no word of the events of the previous evening and of preventing her from speaking to Miss Danville. From there he went into the pantry next door. When the kettle came to the boil, he was waiting for Miss Danville with the bodkin in his hand. If she made any sound when he struck her, the whistle would serve to drown it. He allowed himself one stroke only, because time was short, but it proved sufficient. Then he hurried back to his own room, locking the pantry door behind him.'

Mallett stopped abruptly and gave his moustache points a tug.

'I think that's all,' he said finally.

There was a moment's silence in the room. Then Pettigrew spoke.

'Yes,' he said slowly, 'that's all, so far as Phillips is concerned, poor devil. Do you think, by the way, he meant to dispose of Miss Brown once she was married and insured?'

'That one I can't tell,' said Mallett. 'But I should say it was very likely. There is such a thing as the appetite that grows by what it feeds on, and a successful murderer is a dangerous sort of husband to have, especially if he's interested in life insurance.'

'Yes,' said Pettigrew. 'And he had that five hundred to get back from the Empyrean too – – I was thinking,' he went on, 'Miss Brown knows nothing of the arrest yet?'

'No, sir,' said Jellaby.

'It will be a bad blow to her, I'm afraid.'

Pettigrew became aware that Mallett was staring very hard at him.

'I dare say it will be, Mr Pettigrew,' he said. 'I thought you might like to break the news to her yourself. You never know your luck, you know.'

'Confound your impudence!' said Pettigrew, and getting up he walked quickly out of the police-station.

# CHAPTER NINETEEN

## *Conclusion*

PETTIGREW'S room at the Control had a disagreeably familiar aspect when he entered it. There were three or four fresh files on his desk awaiting his attention. A collection of neat typewritten notes from Miss Brown informed him that various people had telephoned in his absence and wished to speak to him as soon as he returned. Another note, thoughtfully typed in red, stated that the Controller wished to see him as soon as possible on a matter of urgency. Pettigrew pushed them on one side and sat, his chin supported in his hands, staring at the wall opposite. He sat there, immobile, for the space of ten minutes.

Anybody observing him would have said that he was deep in thought. Actually, his mind during this period was as near to being a perfect blank as it had been at any time in his life. It was as though his brain, confronted with a task from which it shrank, had deliberately gone on strike. If there was one thing on which Pettigrew prided himself, it was his capacity for honest, and, if necessary, ruthless self-analysis. For once his power had failed him. He could not bring himself to examine the emotions that he dimly felt at the back of his consciousness. That way, he was aware, lay pain and ridicule beyond bearing. It was much easier to sit staring at the wall, thinking of precisely nothing.

At last he straightened his back and sat up in his chair. He yawned, looked at his watch, was surprised to see how late it was, and then, hastily, as though afraid he would change his mind, pressed the button of the electric bell on his desk.

'Better get it over and done with, I suppose,' he muttered.

Miss Brown came into the room, gave him a civil good afternoon, and sat down on her usual chair, her shorthand pad on her knee and her pencil poised. It might have been any ordinary afternoon at the office, Pettigrew reflected, with an absurd stab of regret for the carefree days when he was new to Marsett Bay. She was looking as neat and composed as usual, he observed, and certainly no paler than she had been when he left to go to Eastbury.

'You can put away your pencil and paper, Miss Brown,' he began in a voice that sounded far rougher than he had intended. 'I'm afraid I have some rather serious news for you.'

She looked up quickly, looked straight at him, and once more her whole face was transfigured by the revelation of these astonishing eyes.

'For me?' she asked.

'Yes. Your – er – Mr Phillips was arrested this morning.'

Her self-control is marvellous, thought Pettigrew. Except for a sharp indrawn breath, she gave no sign of emotion.

'He was arrested for the murder of Miss Danville.'

'Yes. It would be for that, of course.' She spoke very quietly, hardly above a whisper. She was looking away from him now and Pettigrew had the impression that she was speaking to herself rather than to him.

'I'm afraid this must be rather a shock to you,' he went on. She was taking it well, he said to himself, and he ought to be grateful to her for that. He had had enough of feminine emotions at Marsett Bay to last him a lifetime. At the same time, he could not but feel an obscure sense of disappointment. Surely the girl might show a little more emotion! It was unnatural. He had been prepared for anything, but not for this flat calm. From somewhere in the back of his mind floated unbidden a theatrical expression he had heard somewhere: 'The scene went over very flat.'

Miss Brown was speaking and to his ear it seemed that she was picking her words with care.

'Yes,' she said slowly, 'it is a shock – a shock to everybody, I suppose. We – we all knew him so well, didn't we? But after all, anything is better than letting poor Miss Danville's murder' – for the first time her voice quivered a little – 'go unpunished. I couldn't have borne that.'

Pettigrew could not keep a touch of asperity from his voice. 'I think you're a remarkable young woman,' he exclaimed. 'After all this man was – –'

He stopped, feeling thoroughly annoyed with himself for having been betrayed into saying the one thing he had not intended to say. But she seemed in no way offended.

'I wasn't in love with him, you know, Mr Pettigrew,' she said very clearly and distinctly. 'Never at any time.'

'I dare say not,' he retorted. 'But after all, you meant to marry him, and I should have thought – –'

What sort of ridiculous argument was he getting himself into now? he asked himself helplessly.

'No,' said Miss Brown very firmly. 'I did not mean to marry him. He meant to marry me, but that's not the same thing, is it?'

Pettigrew leaned back in his chair.

'This,' he said, 'is extremely interesting.' His voice, at its driest and most judicial, disguised the wholly irrational sense of jubilation which her last words had pro-

uced. 'When did you make up your mind to refuse
im?'

'I never made up my mind to accept him,' Miss Brown
ointed out in her precise fashion. 'But it was only after
Miss Danville's death that I knew for certain that I
ouldn't possibly marry him.'

'Just what does that mean?' I wish, thought Petti-
rew, that I didn't feel as though I were cross-examining
dangerous witness on inadequate instructions, but I
must know. 'Do you mean you knew all the time that he
ad killed her?'

'Good heavens, no!' she answered quickly. 'Nothing
f the sort. How could I? It was simply that after her
eath he seemed to change his nature altogether. I can
understand it now, of course, but it was a shock to me
hen. He had been quiet and reasonable and – gentle is
he only word for it. All at once he became impatient
nd greedy and possessive. He tried to rush me into
marrying him straight away. He pretended to be sorry
bout Miss Danville, but I could see he didn't mean
t. I got the feeling of something vulgar and ugly
oming through the outside surface. Did you ever see
dragon-fly coming out of the skin of its larva? It was
ike that, only the other way round. I just knew I had
early made the most terrible mistake in the world –
vith poor Miss Danville egging me on all the time to
lo it, too!'

'It was because she found out what a mistake it would
ave been that she was killed,' Pettigrew said.

Miss Brown did not appear to have heard him. She
was still pursuing her own line of thought, talking
almost as much to herself as to him.

'Of course, part of the change was in me,' she went on
softly. 'I think I must have grown up quite a lot in the
last three weeks. I realized how very, very stupid I'd

been. Stupid about Tom Phillips, of course, and stupid about Miss Danville and lots of other things.'

What a delicious voice she had when she talked like this, Pettigrew was thinking. Almost as remarkable in its way as her eyes. Strange he had never noticed it before. It was as much to persuade her to go on as for any other reason that he said, 'Other things? Such as – –?'

For once the composed Miss Brown looked uncomfortable and awkward. Looking fixedly at her feet, she flushed distinctly as she muttered, 'Oh . . . love – and marriage – and things in general. It doesn't matter now.'

She stood up to go out.

'Wait a minute,' said Pettigrew, standing up in his turn. 'There's one thing I still don't understand. Before I went to Eastbury you told me you were taking your extra leave at Christmas and didn't expect to be coming back to the Control. I took it for granted you were getting married. Why did you want to leave here?'

Almost sullenly, she answered, 'I didn't want to stay on without Miss Danville.'

'Was that the only reason?'

'It's reason enough, isn't it? What more do you want?'

Miss Brown's composure, maintained so long, was beginning to break down at last. There was a ring of desperation in her voice. Her face was white and drawn and there were tears standing in her eyes. In two strides Pettigrew was round the desk and stood confronting her.

'Was I the reason?' he demanded. 'Did you want to get away from me?'

He seized her hand. The pencil which she still held stuck up grotesquely between their clasped fingers.

'Please! Please don't!' she cried in distress. 'You only make it worse for me. Let me go!'

'Eleanor,' said Pettigrew, speaking very rapidly, 'I am old, I am unattractive, I am unsuccessful. I am crotchety and quirky and set in my ways. I am given to futile little jokes and I have been known to drink too much. I am utterly unfitted to marry anybody, let alone a girl of your age. But I'm damned if I am going to allow it to be said that I let you run away from here because you didn't think I cared for you. I want you desperately, and I want you here. If you go, you go with my malediction on your head, and I promise you solemnly I shall use all my influence with the Ministry of Labour to have you directed into domestic service in a hospital for bombed-out inebriates. Now, what do you say?'

'Frank,' said Eleanor Brown some time later, 'when did you first realize you loved me?'

'To be quite honest, I'm not at all sure. But I think it was something Inspector Mallett said recently that put me in mind of it.'

She laughed contentedly.

'I suppose it was Inspector Mallett who told you my name was Eleanor,' she said.

'No,' said Pettigrew. 'As a matter of fact, that was Inspector Jellaby. Our police are wonderful, aren't they?'

The telephone rang. Miss Brown answered it.

'It's the Controller,' she announced. 'He wants to see you at once. What shall I say?'

'Tell him,' said Pettigrew happily, 'to go and stick pins in himself.'

# THE PERENNIAL LIBRARY MYSTERY SERIES